SIMPATÍA

SIMPATÍA

a novel

RODRIGO BLANCO CALDERÓN

TRANSLATED BY
NOEL HERNÁNDEZ GONZÁLEZ and **DANIEL HAHN**

SEVEN STORIES PRESS
NEW YORK · OAKLAND

Seven Stories Press
140 Watts Street
New York, NY 10013
sevenstories.com

College professors and high school and middle school teachers may order free examination copies of Seven Stories Press titles. Visit https://www.sevenstories.com/pg/resources-academics or email academic@sevenstories.com.

Library of Congress Cataloging-in-Publication Data

Names: Blanco Calderón, Rodrigo, 1981- author. | Hernández González, Noel, translator. | Hahn, Daniel, translator.
Title: Simpatía : a novel / Rodrigo Blanco Calderón ; translated by Noel Hernández González and Daniel Hahn.
Other titles: Simpatía. English
Description: New York : Seven Stories Press, 2024.
Identifiers: LCCN 2023037981 | ISBN 9781644213650 (trade paperback) | ISBN 9781644213667 (ebook)
Subjects: LCSH: Separated people--Fiction. | Inheritance and succession--Fiction. | Life change events--Fiction. | LCGFT: Novels.
Classification: LCC PQ8550.412.L36 S5513 2024 | DDC 863/.7--dc23/eng/20231002
LC record available at https://lccn.loc.gov/2023037981

Printed in the United States of America

9 8 7 6 5 4 3 2 1

To my sister Gabriela,
angel of abandoned dogs

simpatía

from lat. sympathĭa, & this from gr. συμμπάθεια *(sympátheia) "community of feelings."*

   noun. Affective inclination between people, generally spontaneous & mutual.

   noun. Affective inclination toward animals or things, also assumed in some animals.

   noun. The manner of being and character of a person that makes him attractive or agreeable to others.

   noun. Biol. Relationship of pathophysiological activity among organs without direct connection.

   noun. Phys. Relationship between two bodies or systems whereby action of one induces the same behavior in the other.

—Dictionary of the Royal Spanish Academy

I would like, to begin with, to say that though parents, husbands, children, lovers, and friends are all very well, they are not dogs.

—ELIZABETH VON ARNIM

A big dog follows you,
the faithful, slow dog of our estrangement.

—VICENTE GERBASI

I.

1

On the day his wife left the country, Ulises Kan decided to get himself a dog.

When he saw everything from the merciless vantage point that a marriage brings when it ends, it made sense. Before they married, he'd warned her he didn't want children. Paulina had replied that she was allergic to dogs.

Martín, his father-in-law, in the first conversation they'd had shortly after the honeymoon, informed him that, no, his daughter was not allergic to dogs, or dust, or anything.

"If anything, allergic to joy, like her mother. God rest her soul."

Then he let out a loud guffaw. Ulises wanted to laugh, too, but the old man had such a coughing fit that Ulises thought he was dying.

"It's true, it is possible to live without dogs, but there's really no need," Martín said when he had finally caught his breath.

From that day on, Ulises knew his marriage was doomed. Now that he was searching online for information about dog shelters that gave the animals up for adoption, he understood that Martín was right. He'd been right all along.

His father-in-law was "fucking handsome." That's how he'd

described him in imaginary conversations with friends. When the last of these friends moved to Buenos Aires with their family, Ulises left the shared WhatsApp group.

That's how we—those of us who stay behind—leave, he thought.

His father-in-law's beauty was like Alain Delon's. Ulises got the sense that Martín was not only aware of the resemblance, but secretly cultivated it. The abandonment he suffered as a child, the hatred he felt for his children and for women, the idyllic memories of his army days, the dog cemetery in the garden of the house, the addiction to loneliness that only got worse as the end of his life drew nearer. All the distinctive traits of Alain Delon's life, well-documented or otherwise, were echoed in Martín's.

He'd first made the connection on the day the two of them had watched a TV documentary to mark the fiftieth anniversary of Luchino Visconti's *The Leopard*. Delon was interviewed in the Palermo district where the Palazzo Valguarnera-Gangi was located, the same palace where the famous ball scene was filmed.

"There's never been so much beauty in one place: Alain Delon, Claudia Cardinale, and Burt Lancaster," said Martín, counting off the cast with his fingers, as if naming the 1987 Napoli lineup.

Ulises thought that in his father-in-law's life, in some sumptuous room of his past, there must have been a Claudia Cardinale.

Martín snorted when he asked him.

"You ask such dumb questions, Ulises. Of course I have my Claudia Cardinale! And I know that you do too. But even a man who's never had his Claudia Cardinale can still watch

Claudia Cardinale," he said, pointing at the TV screen. "You understand?"

Ulises nodded, though he wasn't sure he did.

He didn't know why his father-in-law had stopped talking to his children. Paulina wasn't sure either and, though she claimed to be over it, deep down she remained bitter. Ulises only got to meet him because he'd really persevered. He thought the idea of just not meeting your father-in-law at all was outrageous. She avoided the subject as long as she could, but one fine day, she drove him to a house next to Los Chorros Park, at the top of a steep cul-de-sac. Ulises had only been once before to that park in the northeast of Caracas, one of the oldest in the city, famous for its waterfalls and springs. The Khans had taken him there for a picnic to celebrate the news of Señora Khan's pregnancy. "You're going to have a baby brother," they told him with a strained smile. Ulises could still recall the silence that engulfed that childhood excursion, only interrupted by the sound of falling water.

"Where is it coming from?" asked Ulises, pointing to a waterfall.

"The water?" said Señor Khan.

"Yes."

"From the Ávila," replied Señor Khan. "From up there."

Ulises looked at the enormous green mass that Señor Khan's arm was pointing at. The mountain-range that guarded the city, its back turned like a sleeping giant.

"I thought *this* was the Ávila," he said.

"No, Ulises. This is Los Chorros Park. The Ávila is further up. But if you go upstream, you do get to the mountain."

On that first visit, when Paulina stopped the car outside a brick house with a black door, she warned him:

"Don't even think about mentioning it."

"Mentioning what?"

"Why we don't talk and all that. He'll get mad at you and throw you out of the house. Well, he still might."

After she'd pulled up and dropped him alone by the door-bell, Ulises felt like Chris O'Donnell about to walk into Al Pacino's cabin in *Scent of a Woman*. But unlike the character in the movie, Martín was cut off from the world not by blindness, but pulmonary emphysema.

"Stage four. I'm fucked," said his father-in-law, by way of greeting.

Martín spent his time watching old movies and reading. His only other hobbies in his retirement were gardening and walking the dogs. Every day, he and Señor Segovia, his chauffeur and right-hand man, would take Michael, Sonny, and Fredo out for a walk. Two German Shepherds and a stray who were, according to him, "quite a sight." They'd drive them in the pickup to a park just before Cota Mil and let them run loose. Sometimes Martín would get out with them. At other times, he preferred to watch from his seat in the truck, following their comings and goings, the jumping, the barking, the growling, and the biting, as if they were running at some crazy racecourse. Martín would always come back home happy, as if he had won, or lost, a bet against himself.

They talked for about six hours on that first afternoon. When Paulina picked him up that night, she couldn't believe it. She wanted to know how her father was, what they'd talked about, how everything had gone.

Ulises attempted a summary, but he wasn't sure how to do it. All he knew was that he'd had a great evening.

"By the way, your father's very handsome," Ulises said. "Now

I know where you get your eyes."

Her expression softened, and, for an instant, Ulises saw the child resurfacing like a drowned girl from the depths of Paulina's face, only to sink back a second later.

"I think it's because I'm an orphan too," said Ulises, almost as an excuse.

"Did you talk about that?"

"No."

"Aw, so poor little orphans just recognize each other, then?"

After thinking about it for a couple of seconds, Ulises answered:

"Yes, I think so."

They drove the rest of the way in silence. As they entered the apartment, Paulina said:

"Sorry."

"Don't worry about it," said Ulises.

"Honestly, thank you for going to see him."

"It's a pleasure. We agreed to meet again next week."

"OK."

"But I won't go if it bothers you."

"Why would it? Just go."

And that's how Ulises Kan became friends with his father-in-law, a man so handsome that he looked like Alain Delon.

2

On the morning of the crucial day, Ulises dreamed of Claudia Cardinale. The actress was reenacting the sequence in *The Leopard* that made her famous, when Alain Delon's character dances with her. In the dream, Claudia Cardinale was also Nadine, and the setting wasn't the Gangi Palace in Palermo, but the cultural center where Ulises ran his film appreciation workshops. The center was actually a bookstore with several classrooms on the floor above. Claudia, or Nadine, was holding a cellphone.

"What are you doing here?" Ulises asked her.

"You called me," she replied, showing him the phone. He looked at the device held out by a corseted woman in a Garibaldi-era dress and didn't understand a thing.

Ulises read the text message from himself, to her, that just said: *Come.* Then they began to make love.

He woke up crying, and with a huge erection. It was almost nine in the morning. Paulina had left for the office a while ago. He wiped his tears and took a cold shower.

While drinking his first coffee, he logged onto Twitter and checked the news. A student had been killed overnight by the paramilitary groups on Francisco de Miranda Avenue. April had barely begun, but it already was threatening to conclude like a ripe pomegranate: loaded with arils drowned in their own blood. Ulises lingered over the photo of the boy's mother bawling her eyes out, but he couldn't stop thinking about his own tears when he'd woken up. The dream had been interrupted when they were making love. Was that what he was crying about? Maybe. Although, if he'd been crying because of the interruption, there must have been some moment of consciousness when he'd understood it was all a dream. The juxtaposition of the dress and cellphone, perhaps? The truth was that, on one side of the mirror, so to speak, there was Nadine's body. On the other side, his own body between the sheets of that oversized bed, and his tears.

He started reading Borges's essay "The Flower of Coleridge," and wasted his morning jumping from place to place in his old green copy of the *Obras Completas*, like a bumblebee buzzing distractedly around the foothills of a mountain. Around midday, he opened his notebook and penned a title: The Penis of Coleridge. He was about to write a few pages of whatever thoughts he had, when he received Paulina's text: *I'm leaving the country. I can't take it anymore.*

Ulises looked at the phone screen for a while. The screen would go dark, and he would touch it again to make sure the text was still there.

Come, he would have liked to have written to Nadine that time, but he didn't.

Instead, he replied to Paulina: *OK.*

To which Paulina answered straight away: *I want to leave by myself, Ulises. Do you understand what I'm saying?*

Ulises didn't take long to get back to her: *I do, Paulina. That's how it'll be. We'll talk about it tonight.*

He needed to look for Nadine. That much was clear now. But what if he couldn't find her? Or she didn't reply?

This time, it was Paulina who took a little while to get back to him: *Thank you.*

They couldn't divorce straight away, as they hadn't yet been married for five years—they'd only just had their fourth anniversary. The best thing to do, Paulina told him when she arrived that evening, was to sign a legal separation and give a lawyer power of attorney to complete the divorce a year later.

"Since the apartment is under my name," said Paulina, "I'll deal with the process of selling it, and the fees for the lawyer, who's a family friend. You'd get ten percent of whatever money we make from the sale, if that's alright. You can stay till we find a buyer. Actually, you do the viewings. You can keep the car, too."

Ulises accepted. In return, Paulina only asked him to deal with her father and arrange for her to see him before she left.

After that conversation, Ulises visited Martín and, without beating around the bush, told him about the divorce and Paulina's trip.

"She's leaving in a couple of months. Three at the most. She begged me to ask you to see her before she leaves, please."

"No," said the old man and he turned up the volume on the TV.

Ulises waited a few seconds and tried again.

"Paulina is in a real state," he lied.

"Look, Ulises," Martín said suddenly, turning off the TV, "I'll tell you just once so it's totally clear. The apartment where you two live is mine, not Paulina's. Do you want to stay there after she goes?"

Ulises felt his throat drying up.

"Well, do you want to or don't you?" Martín insisted.

"I do," he said at last.

"Great. As far as I'm concerned, you go right on living there as long as you want. But if you ever mention this whole Paulina thing again, I'll put you right out on the street. Understood?"

"Understood."

Ulises guessed it was time to end the visit. However, as if nothing had happened, Martín asked him:

"Have you read Elizabeth von Arnim?"

"Who?"

"Elizabeth von Arnim."

"No."

"Me neither, but I was told about her once and I've never forgotten it. She was an Australian writer, very famous in her time. Toward the end, she wrote her memoirs, called *All the Dogs of My Life*. Apparently, that's all she talks about. The story of every dog she ever had. She doesn't talk about her husbands, children, or lovers. Just her dogs. Pretty terrific, isn't it?"

"It is," said Ulises.

"Let's go outside," said Martín. "Al jardín!" and he stood up.

Ulises had wanted to see the famous garden ever since he learned his father-in-law had a dog cemetery there. So far, all he'd seen of the house had been the front room, the wide staircase that led to the second floor and this bedroom where Martín received him. One time, he'd gotten lost after going to the bathroom on the landing, and ended up in the library. A room with a high ceiling, its walls covered with shelves full of books. And between each shelf and the next, and in the space between their top and the ceiling, the largest collection of portraits of El Libertador Simón Bolívar he had ever seen.

The garden was huge. The far end was at the foot of a mountain that belonged to Los Chorros Park. Garden and park were separated by a thin metallic fence that looked from here like a spiderweb.

"Aren't you afraid?" asked Ulises, pointing to the back of the garden.

"Of what?"

"Of someone coming into the garden through there. Or that a huge downpour is going to bring the mountain down."

Martín smiled.

"When Caracas sinks—which it will—the peak of that mountain is the only thing that'll survive. Besides, there's a Guardia Nacional post in the park, and they patrol all the time. I got them to install it years ago, when I bought the house."

The garden was divided into two sections. One huge area, where Michael, Sonny, and Fredo roamed free, marked out by an internal fence with a gate, just a meter or so high, which the dogs respected with mysterious obedience. And another part, much smaller, hidden behind a row of irregularly trimmed bushes, also with a gate, which was the resting place of the remains of the dogs who'd died over the last few years.

There were four graves. Four little parcels of flattened soil, each with a sea stone and a small wooden plaque. The plaques had the name of the dogs and the dates of their death.

"Ying-Ying, Chirú, Oreo, and Chobi," said Martín.

His father-in-law seemed calm.

"When did you start with this cemetery thing?"

Martín sighed and said:

"On the day I understood that, despite all the evidence to the contrary, God might in fact exist. One day I saw my dogs and, through them, I thought I saw God, and that's when I knew. Sadly, I realized it very late."

"And your wife, how did she feel about this?"

"My wife?"

"Paulina's mamá. How did she feel about the dog cemetery?"

"And what do you care what Paulina's mother did or didn't think about the cemetery? It's got nothing to do with what I'm telling you."

"I'm sorry. I don't know why I said that."

"Or maybe it is connected, come to think of it. Those priests in the Middle Ages turned out to be right. Women are the opposite of dogs: they are the living proof that the devil also exists."

"Do you really think so, Martín?"

"Of course I do. Look at Paulina, for example."

"What's wrong with her?"

"Haven't you noticed, Ulisito?"

"Noticed what?"

"She's losing her mind over the whole inheritance thing. She's afraid I'll die and leave her with nothing. The apartment is what she wants, so she can sell it. And leave you on the street without a cent, like a dog."

3

Paulina left in the last week of June, and the next time Ulises saw her in Caracas was in early September, when General Martín Ayala died.

The wake was in the Cementerio del Este. Ulises walked into the chapel, apprehensive about encountering the stiff image of his father-in-law. But the atmosphere was so tense it made him forget his fear. The few mourners stood in two groups on either side of the urn. They were military men in full uniform. The weird thing was that the groups didn't communicate. Nobody crossed from left to right or vice versa. They looked at each other as if divided by a river they *might* cross at any moment, with an infantry charge, to take the enemy bank.

Ulises moved closer and stopped before the urn. He heard some murmuring behind him.

"The son-in-law, I think," someone said in a whisper that everybody could hear.

He stood with his head bowed, watching his father-in-law's petrified face, feigning a self-absorption that was impossible to feel in that rarefied air. Two minutes later, he straightened up, took a few steps aside, and started to read the ribbons on the wreaths.

To General Martín Ayala, a brave soldier of the country.
Our condolences to family and friends. Academia Militar de
Caracas. To General M. Ayala Ayala. Cornerstone of the Ven-
ezuelan Army. Academia Militar de la Aviación Bolivariana,
Edo. Aragua. In loving memory of our illustrious comrade.
Sociedad Bolivariana de Caracas. Always in our heart. The
Hotel Humboldt Workers' Association.

Hotel Humboldt?, Ulises wondered.

He felt someone grabbing his arm. It was Señor Segovia.

"The girl has just arrived," he said pointing outside.

Ulises looked lost.

"Señora Paulina," said Segovia.

"Of course," said Ulises, and he went out to the main hall.

She looked devastated. Her features seemed eroded from within, as if caused by the kind of soil extraction that precedes subsidence. He tried to act with the same intimacy as when they lived together, that almost fraternal and slightly sad intimacy of couples who have not yet quite separated. But she put a stop to that.

"Don't be a hypocrite."

"What are you talking about, Pauli?" answered Ulises, turning pale. He thought about Nadine. There was no way Señor Segovia could have told her anything. Perhaps Carmen, the maid?

"I'm going to contest the will. Don't think you'll get away with it."

She turned her back on him and entered the chapel.

Martín had left Ulises the apartment.

The previous day, his father-in-law's lawyer had informed him that Martín had just passed away and he asked him to come into the office as a matter of urgency. He was a young man, probably his age. There, he gave him a copy of the part of the will that concerned him.

"Is this for real?" Ulises asked.

"It is. There's just one condition. General Ayala requested that you coordinate a special project as a prerequisite of your becoming the apartment's owner. If you carry this out within the established timeframe, Señor Kan, the property is yours."

Martín had arranged to donate Los Argonautas, the main house, to a foundation dedicated to rescuing abandoned dogs. Ulises was tasked with coordinating, together with the couple in charge of the foundation, its proper setup and operation in the grounds of the house.

"Within 120 days after his death. That's about four months. Counting from today, the foundation must be up and running by January 3 next year at the latest," said the lawyer.

"But, why me?" was all Ulises could ask.

The lawyer shrugged and said:

"Señor Martín left a sum to guarantee the foundation would be economically supported for several years. I'll take care of that."

Ulises processed all this and asked another question:

"Did Martín leave anything to Paulina and her brother?"

"Why do you want to know?"

"No reason. It's just that all this is going to get me in trouble with them, as you can understand."

"I can. You needn't worry. Señor Martín's children will be well taken care of."

"Thank God. Though they're not going to like this one bit. Paulina doesn't like dogs, you see."

The lawyer gave a hint of a smile.

"That apartment could make you a small fortune, if you wait for prices to go up. But the house is something else, that's the crown jewel. If you ever have legal problems because of this matter of the inheritance, please contact me."

"OK," he said.

"Great. In this folder you'll find all the documents about the foundation. Everything you need is in here, as well as the contact details for the Galíndez family, they're the couple in charge. I'd recommend getting in touch with them as soon as possible."

"I will," said Ulises.

4

The Simpatía por el Perro Foundation had been established three years prior to Señor Martín's death, and some months after that of Amparito—Jesús and Mariela's little daughter. To start with, the foundation consisted of a support network with a presence on Twitter, Facebook, and Instagram. Jesús was a dog trainer and Mariela a vet. They'd post information on social media about stray and abandoned dogs that were being given up for adoption. Often, these were dogs they'd rescued themselves, and taken to the shelters and veterinary clinics they tended to work with. The dogs were looked after there, and they'd try to find them a home. They scraped by on their followers' donations, whether that was food or cash, which at least allowed them to carry on with the project.

Things started to get tough as the crisis and hunger intensified. Everyone who could, left the country. The luckiest did so by plane, many without looking back. When they had bought their tickets and the authorities signed off their papers; when they had sold off the family home at a quarter of its value; when they had left their jobs and done the last round of doctors' visits; when they had already taken the children out of school, even mid-semester, because there was no time to lose;

when everything was ready, then they'd take the car one last time and drive to a faraway park. There they'd pull over, open the back door from the inside and let out the dogs, and when the dogs ran out, mad with joy, they would slam the back door shut, speed away and escape.

The number of dogs Jesús and Mariela rescued skyrocketed during that last year. The usual clinics and shelters couldn't cope. They started taking them to their own house in the El Paraíso development. Dogs of all breeds, ages, and sizes. Well-fed dogs, malnourished dogs, puppies, old dogs riddled with cancer and mange. A sad and scattered pack that was turning the city into a war hospital.

At some point, the press picked up on what was happening. First was a feature on the more than fifty horses that died of mange in the Santa Rita Hippodrome, in the west of the country. The photographs showed the horses' remains: the bulging eyes numb to the clouds of flies, and the ribcages, and the wire netting that was the bones under the strips of skin. After that came the story of Rosenda, the elephant at Caricuao Zoo, whose flesh hung like threadbare stage curtains over a meager body that could barely move. And finally, the dogs. Strays that quite a few madmen had started killing and eating right there on the street. And domestic ones, who had been abandoned by their owners in some park or tied, with no food or water, to the fence of some factory, parking lot, or garage, taking advantage of the deathly loneliness of the weekends.

April saw the sparking of student protests, and things got worse. Caught in the crossfire of clashes between the Army and demonstrators, donations became scarce. Several of their dogs died for lack of food or medicine. By June, the Army had already killed over a hundred young people, imprisoned another thousand, and managed to dissolve any attempt at protesting. Now they were hunting down "conspirators" in their own homes, relying on denunciations by neighbors linked to the Communal Councils of the Venezuelan Revolution.

Los Verdes, in the El Paraíso development, was a huge residential complex that for the past week had been bombarded with tear gas fired by the military from the highway. At first, they claimed it was because several of the youths involved with the protests lived there. And by the end of the third day, they had indeed arrested over twenty in an operation that lasted hours and was widely reported in the media.

However, what really made an impact on the night of the arrests was the killing of Thor, a mixed-breed dog who lived in one of the apartments they raided. The dog started barking when he saw the soldiers coming into the house, so one of them shot him with a pellet gun. Jesús and Mariela lived in a house in the La Odila area, near the Brígido Iriarte Stadium, just minutes from Los Verdes. Somebody gave Thor's owners their number, and at one in the morning, the couple were woken by the ringing of the doorbell and shouting.

The pellet shot had blown out Thor's eye and some brain matter. Jesús believed that something could still be done since, despite it all, and wailing with pain, Thor still occasionally looked at them with his remaining eye and showed a spark of eagerness. It was Mariela who, having extracted the shrapnel, told him there was just too much damage. The owners had had to leave, to go to the local command HQ, where the military had taken their son. Mariela phoned the woman on the number she'd been given, told her about the situation and asked her permission to put the dog to sleep.

It was all over by five in the morning. They put Thor's corpse in a bag to take to one of the clinics to be cremated.

Then Mariela burst into tears and said to her husband:

"I can't take it any longer. Let's just get away from all this shit, please."

And they would have left the country, abandoning the few dogs they'd saved from the wreckage to their own fate, had it not been for the strange call they received a few days later: a retired air force officer, General Martín Ayala Ayala, was inviting them to his house.

5

That call was just one of many things going on. The wave of indignation provoked by Thor's killing didn't stop the bombardment of the Los Verdes residential complex from continuing at a regular rate: four hours in the morning, four in the afternoon and another two in the evening. The neighbors expected more raids, but they never materialized. As the days went by, the hundreds of empty teargas canisters overflowed from the hard shoulder on the highway, and still no one knew why the siege was continuing.

Then one morning, the riot squad wasn't on the highway anymore, and the bombardment stopped.

Something similar happened with Nadine. Ever since Paulina's departure a couple of weeks earlier, Ulises had been daily postponing the moment when he would try to find her. He spent his days looking at photos of puppies offered up for adoption, without making up his mind. Until one afternoon it was she who called him and, just like that, her years of absence evaporated.

"Hello," said Nadine.

That particle of breath was all it took for Ulises to recognize her.

"Where are you?" he asked.

"In Caracas."

Such a vague answer would have been absurd in the years before the exodus. Now, however, it was a whisper in his ear.

"And you?" asked Nadine.

"At home. Do you remember the address?"

"I do."

"Come, then."

Come, repeated Ulises after hanging up. Four years to say that word that he'd swallowed and which had remained buried in the humus of his chest like a still living bird.

When Ulises opened his apartment door and let her in, they threw themselves onto each other hungrily. Nadine came quite quickly. Her orgasm wasn't one of those stones that falls in the water and spreads into waves. It was more like the burning heat of an axe, brief and rough, cutting through wood with a single stroke. Almost without pleasure. Ulises hurried and buried his cock deep inside her. He didn't move until he felt the last drop leaving him, his blood turning into hot snow.

Then they lay there, side by side, staring at the ceiling, their breathing in synch. Nadine didn't ask after Paulina, she didn't even check the time, or worry about a sudden interruption. Ulises didn't stop to think whether he should have finished inside her. Their bodies had long since become caves awaiting a nocturnal animal.

After a while, they talked. They said things to each other. They exchanged short phrases as if these were misplaced items of clothing. They covered their skin with vague words that underlined what they already knew: they were together now. In this way, Ulises confirmed that Paulina had left the country.

And Nadine that she was on the pill. She did not have a boyfriend, but she did have polycystic ovaries.

Nadine had been living in Buenos Aires. There she'd done a Master's in contemporary dance and tried to establish herself as a dancer. Things didn't work out, so she decided to return to Venezuela.

"But this place is a mess, Nadine," said Ulises.

"I know, but you're here."

That was when Ulises started to look at her closely. He saw some premature wrinkles. He also noticed a single gray lock that divided her hair in two. On the other hand, her body looked smooth, apart from a scar on her stomach. Maybe it was a dancer thing, as if their heads and bodies came from different people, the two parts relating to each other like Dorian Gray and his picture, but the other way round. Since dancers, Ulises thought, don't tend to use makeup and their faces clearly show the passing of time, whereas their bodies, always young, hide their secret pact.

Ulises told her he was still running workshops at the same cultural center, but it was increasingly difficult to find new students.

"Everyone's leaving."

"And how do you get by?"

For a moment he considered lying and mentioning some savings in dollars, or having sold his car, something like that.

"To tell you the truth, I'm supported by my father-in-law. Or my ex-father-in-law," he said.

And in broad strokes, he told her the story of his relationship with Martín.

"I'd like to meet him," said Nadine.

"That's impossible."

"Why's that? Didn't you say he hates Paulina?"

"He hates women in general."

"I'm sure his wife was a witch."

"I don't know. I love the old man, but you can tell he's a piece of work."

"He's giving us the apartment and our food. I've got to take his side."

"Giving *us*?"

"I'm fucking with you, idiot," Nadine said suddenly, with a strong Argentinian accent.

Ulises sat up, kissed her, and started slowly to move across her body, finding his way through that forest of seasons aided just by the tip of his nose. He recognized the smell of dead leaves between her tiny breasts. The aroma of rice milk between her thighs. Under her arms, after carefully extending them, the scent of a closet with freshly washed clothes. The gnarled feet, tortured by dancing, shining marble-like.

I must be delirious, thought Ulises.

Every kiss and every sniff of Nadine's skin were like bites of madness whisking him off to dreamland.

6

"Claudia's back," announced Ulises.

"Who?" asked Martín without looking away from the TV.

Ulises hadn't come to see Martín the previous week and decided to tell him the truth.

"My Claudia Cardinale. She's back."

Martín looked at him for the first time since he arrived, returned to the TV screen for a few seconds, and then said:

"Holy shit. Well, congrats, Ulisito," and he let out one of his loud guffaws that threatened to drown him.

"You don't mind, Martín?"

"Why would I?"

"Because of Paulina, I guess."

"Ulises, please—don't be an asshole. What's her name?"

"Nadine."

"Nice. Is she French?"

"Her mamá is."

"And when are you bringing her over for me to meet her?"

Nadine thought being invited over by Martín was quite normal. Could the old man have been behind the whole thing?, Ulises wondered. No, there was no way. Nobody knew about Nadine. It's true she'd been to the apartment once, when he had the terrible idea of inviting over his friends from the cultural center. Paulina decided to invite her friends from the office at the same time, a larger and noisier group. Both groups, like soccer teams with a hangover, hardly faced up against each other at all. Each occupied their own half of the field and just passed the ball amongst themselves without surprises. At night, when they were alone again and clearing up the dishes, Paulina didn't even mention Nadine. Or any of his other guests, really.

"That was fun, wasn't it?" was all she said.

"Lots of fun," said Ulises.

A few minutes later they went to their bedroom, turned off the lights, and went to sleep.

Yet Martín was a very powerful man, Ulises kept thinking. Paulina never went into details, but his father-in-law had had links to Chávez himself ever since the latter's years at the Academia Militar. It was an ambiguous relationship, since Martín had also been a key figure in the suppression of Chávez's attempted coup on February 4, 1992. He retired in 1999. In the years that followed, the Bolivarian Revolution had taken over the country. After the coup against Chávez on April 11, 2002, and his return to power two days later, there'd been a purge of the Fuerzas Armadas, Petróleos de Venezuela, and the Corte Suprema de Justicia. The prosecution reached several retired officials, but General Martín Ayala remained untouchable throughout this time, and even afterwards.

How could he be sure Martín hadn't ordered a tail on him in the weeks before he'd married Paulina? But even if he had, what could that hypothetical spy have seen? Until then, his relationship with Nadine had been limited to going for an occasional coffee at the cultural center on the days he taught his course. Often, they'd go with other teachers, students, and customers from the bookstore. He had also exchanged a few text messages from which some special interest might be inferred, but nothing too compromising. The key to their relationship had been in their glances. Or in those extra seconds that they spent in their hello and goodbye hugs.

A week before his marriage, Ulises had stayed behind after class. Henry, the coordinator at the cultural center, had asked him to lock up, because he had an important dinner that day. Ulises waited for the next-door class to finish their Friday poetry workshop. Henry's office was on the second floor, like the classrooms. In the office, he had a shelf full of accounting books and a desk with a heavy split-screen monitor where one could watch the CCTV.

Ulises, who was getting bored, left the classroom and went to Henry's office. He sat in his chair and looked at the screen. In the lower left-hand corner, which relayed images from the camera trained on the bookstore cash register, he saw Nadine. She was reading in her corner, alone, as the store had already closed. He thought it strange that she hadn't left yet. Ulises took a photo of the screen and sent it to her on WhatsApp.

I'm watching you, he wrote in English.

Nadine interrupted her reading and checked her phone. She smiled and looked for the camera that was watching her. She pulled a silly face and answered:

Hahaha. You pervert!

Yes, I am!! What are you still doing here?

Nothing, I'm reading. I don't feel like leaving just yet. And you?

Oh, OK. I'm waiting for the guy in the poetry workshop to finish. You know how intense he gets.

Hahaha. Yeah.

Henry asked me to lock up.

Ah, OK.

Yep . . . Well, keep reading.

Seriously, Ulises wondered, that was really the most brilliant thing he could come up with? Ask her if she wants to go for a beer later. No, not that, it wasn't wise for them to be seen together around there. So tell her to come up to Henry's office once the poetry workshop is over. Tell her that from there they can watch whatever the CCTV picks up, but that there are no cameras in the office. Tell her, *Come upstairs now.* Tell her, *Come, Nadine.* Just tell her anything but *Keep reading.*

Ulises got up, went back to the classroom, and continued reading, or at least trying to read, a book about TV series and Shakespeare. Or rather claiming that TV series were the new Shakespeare. At first, he was shocked by the suggestion, but wasn't he behaving like Prince Hamlet himself? To call her, or not to call her. Was there really something between them or was it all a misunderstanding created by the ghost of love? Didn't David Foster Wallace say that every love story is a ghost story? Was he only referring to the memory of what's been experienced, or could it also apply to what hasn't happened yet?

The door of the other classroom opened and the students from the poetry workshop started to leave. Ulises got up and spent a little while chatting with the workshop leader. Then they said goodbye and the teacher went down the stairs that led to the bookstore and then out to the street. Ulises listened for a few seconds to the silence that fell again over the murmur of the nighttime traffic. He walked slowly back to Henry's office, sat in his chair again and looked at the screen. Nadine was still there. She wasn't reading a book anymore. She was just looking at her phone.

Come, was all he needed to write. Without adding a single

word more. If she came up, it'd be happiness. If she suddenly left, or even if she answered with a question or some silly comment, then all was lost. But how could all be lost for someone who was getting married in a week?

The minutes went by, and Nadine continued to check her phone, while Ulises stared at the screen, hypnotized. Then Nadine got up from the stool she had behind the cash register, looked into the camera for a moment, and walked toward the bathroom.

She's leaving, Ulises thought. It's now or never.

Nadine came out of the bathroom but went right back to her seat. She stayed there for a few minutes, not even checking her phone. After a while, she got to her feet again, picked up her bag, turned off the bookstore lights, and left.

Ulises went on watching the monitor for another half-hour. In the dark, the cameras barely captured the lighter outlines of bookshelves and furniture.

When he got back to the apartment, Paulina wasn't there. In the weeks leading up to the wedding, they hardly saw each other. Paulina said she was very busy between work and the wedding preparations, which thankfully she had forbidden him from meddling in. She'd take care of everything. As a result, because of the effort she was putting in, she would get drunk with her friends every evening. Ulises wondered if he should be jealous. He roamed around that huge, elegant apartment, even bigger for a couple who had just moved in and weren't planning to have dogs or children. In the end, was that what it was all about? Was that the price to pay? Is that how it had been for him? Since when? And what was she getting out of choosing him?

He didn't know, since they never discussed these things. And some marriages are made for not discussing certain things.

That night, he went to bed thinking about Nadine, a woman so different from the one about to become his wife. Why had he not dared? Why such certainty about the inevitability of heartbreak, and not about attaining his heart's desire? I should have texted her, he said to himself for the umpteenth time. And he fell asleep amid murmurs and recriminations before Paulina got back.

On Monday, when he got to the cultural center, he found a very flustered Henry working behind the till. Nadine had called that morning to say she quit.

7

Any suspicion of a plot hatched behind Ulises' back was dissipated as soon as Nadine and Martín were introduced. They hit it off immediately. They were like close friends, although the happiness they radiated really came from that stupor that marks a true friendship at the moment of its birth. The moment one feels like asking the other person, almost as if in reproach, How come I've lived all this time without meeting you?

When Ulises excused himself to go to the bathroom, the others barely even registered. As he came out again, he heard laughter coming from the bedroom. On the landing, he walked a few steps in the opposite direction and soon found himself in the library. He browsed the books. There were encyclopedias, procedural codes, collections of classics produced by some Spanish publisher during the Franco dictatorship. The rest consisted of a considerable number of tomes bound in leather that used to be blue, now covered by a thick layer of dust.

He looked at all the portraits and drawings of Simón Bolívar and one in particular caught his eye. Since this was on the strip of wall above the bookshelves, just inches from the ceiling, he needed a chair. The image showed Bolívar on a horse, leaning to his right, his outstretched arm stroking something that looked like a pony at first, but which he then identified as a huge dog. It was black, its back covered in white hair. To one side there was a boy in a poncho, with the Andean páramo as a backdrop. He looked for the picture's caption and confirmed it was Bolívar's famous dog, Nevado.

Only now did he register the book that was directly in his line of vision. Its thick white spine stood out among the dark blue row of other volumes. He took it out and looked closely at the cover. He climbed off the chair, sat down, and read the title again: *Collected Works of Elizabeth von Arnim*. He checked the index and found the title that Martín had mentioned: *All the Dogs of My Life*. He knew enough English to understand the title at least. Perhaps Nadine could read it. He took the book with him, returned to the bathroom, and stored it away on a shelf under the sink. He came out again and headed for the bedroom. Nadine and Martín turned to see him come in, then went on talking.

Martín kept raising his voice and laughing. Nadine didn't speak much, but everything she said was intelligent or funny. She never stopped smiling. Ulises watched them in silence. There was a pause and suddenly Martín went red. His neck, cheeks and ears were alight, glowing with alarming intensity.

Seeing this, Ulises started to go red, too.

"What's wrong with you both?" asked Nadine, herself feeling hot.

Martín put an end to it all with one of his suicidal guffaws.

When he had caught his breath, he wiped his tears away with a handkerchief and said with a smile:

"Enough messing about. Let's go outside. Al jardín!"

Michael, Sonny, and Fredo came running from the back of the garden. Nadine not only didn't flinch, but opened the inner gate and went in without even asking. Just like Martín, the dogs greeted her as if they had been waiting for her for a long time.

Dogs never question the love they feel. Why hadn't he asked Nadine to come up to Henry's office that night at the bookstore? Or, even better, why hadn't he gone to her, knowing that she'd been waiting for him? Why hadn't he gone down and lain at her feet, licking them and wagging his ass from side to side, begging her to love him? All those years wasted, for what?

Martín took Nadine's hand and began to show her round the garden with regal restraint. The place was not only huge, as he'd thought when he first saw it, but also placid and beautiful. Two stone pathways circled the lawn, which had been cleared of stubble. An oasis of flowers opened up like an island of color amid the green. Ulises had had to wait four years for Martín to take him there. Still, that was almost nothing compared to the eight years he'd had to wait at the orphanage for his adoptive family, the Khans, to appear.

Well, that's quite an improvement, Ulises thought sarcastically.

He walked to the back of the field. The fence separating it from Los Chorros Park was flimsy and a bit rickety. Ulises heard the murmur of the waterfalls and closed his eyes. He pictured himself naked, swimming in the ice-cold water that flowed down the mountains.

He heard footsteps on the lawn.

"The sound of the water is nice, isn't it?" said Martín.

"It is," said Ulises and he looked out toward the mountain peak.

"That sound was one of the reasons I bought the house. That and the library. My wife, however, was especially taken by the garden. At first, it looked like an abandoned soccer field, and just see what she did with it. All I've done has been to preserve that."

"How long have you been here?"

"Since '99, when I retired. I bought it off General Pinzón's daughter, he was my mentor. In the seventies, he'd gather a group of his best students together and teach us the history of Bolívar in the very same library you already know, the one with all those awful drawings. The true history, of course."

How did he know Ulises had already been to the library? Maybe Señor Segovia told him. Had he seen him taking the book and hiding it? But when exactly? He would need to ask Nadine.

"You lucky bastard. What a delightful girl you've gotten yourself," said Martín.

"I know," said Ulises.

Just then, Nadine's eyes sought them out. The dogs were surrounding her, and with a word from her started running toward them.

"Shall we show her the cemetery?" asked Ulises.

Martín seemed surprised by the question.

"No, Ulisito. That was just for you."

Ulises felt his eyes welling up, and as Nadine came closer, he told her:

"We need to get going."

"Yes, go, go," said Martín and he bent down to pick up a soil-covered tennis ball. He threw the ball into the middle of the garden and the dogs ran after it. Martín followed the dogs, raising his arm in a goodbye.

They walked toward the front door, but just before leaving, Ulises stopped.

"What's wrong?" asked Nadine.

"Let me go to the bathroom for a second. I'll be right back."

8

Nadine didn't know who Señor Segovia was. Only Señora
Carmen had interrupted them while Ulises was in the bathroom.

"How long did I take?" Ulises asked.

"I don't know. An hour?"

"That long? What did you talk about all that time?"

"About the family, I think."

"He's a real character. And he looks good, doesn't he? He's a
very handsome man."

"Very," said Nadine.

"We can go back again next week."

"No. You go."

"Why? You can tell he adores you."

"He's lovely, but there's something I don't like."

"Did something happen?"

"There's something about that family I don't like."

"What do you mean, the family, if you only met the old man?"

"Tell me about them."

"There isn't much to tell. There's Paulina. There's the mamá,
who died some years ago. I never got to meet her. And Paul, the
brother, who lives in Amsterdam."

"Paul and Paulina?"

"They're twins."

"And what's he like?"

"I don't know him."

"He didn't come to the wedding?"

"No. From Pauli's family it was just an aunt, a sister of her late mother's. In the end, only a few people came, but it was fine. We had an amazing honeymoon, that's for sure. Istanbul, London, Porto."

"That's not normal, Ulises."

Ulises hesitated for a few seconds.

"I don't know if it's normal or not. I never had a family."

"But you told me you were adopted."

"Yeah, but they didn't become *my* family."

Ulises had been abandoned as a newborn at the doors of the San Antonio María Claret church on Avenida Rómulo Gallegos. The priests raised him until he was eight, when at last a family showed up wanting to adopt him. It was a couple who had been trying unsuccessfully to have a child for years. The fact that Ulises was the same age as their marriage was seen as a sign from fate. A gift from God to make up for time lost.

"The problem was, the woman got pregnant just a few months after I moved in with them. Ironic, isn't it? After that, they never quite knew what to do with me."

"It's weird."

"What's weird?"

"I was just thinking it must be weird having a surname that doesn't mean anything to you."

"The original surname is Khan, with a H. They were from Guyana City and then moved to Caracas. They left the country some years ago. Señor Khan came from a family in Trinidad with Hindu heritage. I got rid of the H."

"What for?"

"It sounds better."

"The H is silent."

"Fine, well, it looks better. And to me it sounds better, too. Ulises Kan sounds a bit like James Caan, don't you think?"

"Oh, I see, so that's why. I never understood why you ran workshops about those kinds of movies."

"James Caan is a great actor. The best and worst thing that could have happened to him was taking on the role of Sonny Corleone."

"'A poet trapped in a gangster's body.' Something like that, right?"

"Exactly. His part in *Misery* was his atonement for having played Sonny."

"You know, I found your fascination with him so charming that I stayed in your workshop just for that."

"I'm sorry it was so terrible."

"Look on the bright side. Henry ended up offering me the job at the bookstore. And five years on, here we are."

"Well, four and a half."

"Either way. Too long for you to realize that I liked you."

Paulina and Nadine had both enrolled in the workshops.

"You know, slow but unsteady."

"Silly. Want to watch a movie?"

"You haven't told me why you don't like Martín's family."

Nadine was stroking her body absentmindedly. Her hands going up and down between her breasts and the top of her thighs. Without realizing, Ulises had begun to make the same movements over his own body. And they kept talking that way, caressing themselves, stretching out the beads of sweat like clay.

"Because it reminds me of my own," said Nadine getting up. She went to the bathroom.

All of a sudden, Ulises remembered his first conversation with Martín. James Caan was one of his father-in-law's favorite actors. Ulises was quick to tell him how he'd met Paulina at one of his cinematographic appreciation workshops, the one on James Caan.

"It was that same year. I know that for you, and everyone else really, the marriage must have seemed like madness, kind of rushed, but what can I say? These things happen. It was love at first sight."

Martín listened to him as if he were speaking gibberish.

"What did you make of James Caan's character in *Dogville*? To me, it was like Sonny Corleone had gotten reincarnated as Nicole Kidman's father, killing all those sons of bitches. Fucking great, that movie."

That answer confirmed to him that it wasn't hatred his father-in-law felt toward his own daughter. Or toward the twins, because Paulina stressed that it was the same thing with both of them. But something worse. Martín's hatred was the tension arising from a deeper feeling: an almost total alienation from his own children.

Nadine came out of the bathroom and Ulises asked her:

"Fancy watching *The Godfather*?"

"Always."

"But listen. Let's watch the whole trilogy, right through till dawn."

"Why?"

"I'm thinking about what Francis Ford Coppola said. About how *The Godfather* isn't just a story about gangsters and the Mafia. It's the story of a family."

9

Jesús was not keen on accepting the invitation from the so-called general. If anything, he wanted to file a complaint.

"A complaint about what?" said Mariela.

"I don't know. Harassment. Persecution. Whatever."

"We don't know if it's about Thor. And anyway, file a complaint with who?"

Jesús stopped pacing around and said:

"Course that's what it's about."

The news of Thor's killing had provoked widespread indignation and the mobilizing of several animal welfare organizations. Some personalities abroad such as Arturo Pérez-Reverte and Fernando Vallejo were quick to condemn the little dog's killing on their Twitter accounts. Straight away, journalists linked to the government denied the news, so Thor's owner said that if they didn't believe her, they could check with "the well-known Simpatía por el Perro Foundation," where her pet had been cared for.

The following day, a couple of officers from SEBIN, the political police, showed up at Jesús and Mariela's house. Without presenting a warrant, they came in to check the house and "find out what had happened." Mariela was hesitant, but

Jesús spoke to them and answered all their questions. Even when they asked for the address of the clinic where they'd taken the dog's corpse.

The officers took notes and, on their way out, they reminded them they must stay in Caracas so that they could remain available.

"Excuse me, officer, but available for what?" asked Jesús.

"For the investigation," said the fatter of the officers, the only one who had talked during the visit. "We still need to find out who really did kill the dog."

"I'm telling you, the dog arrived without an eye and its head was shattered by pellets," said Jesús. "There was nothing to be done."

"That's for us to decide. Fingers crossed that the clinic haven't cremated the little dog yet. We might need an autopsy."

"An autopsy?" asked Mariela, who couldn't hold back a nervous giggle.

"Of course. We can't rule out any hypothesis. Malpractice, for example," said the fat policeman, giving her a wink.

Mariela panicked when they'd gone.

"They'll send us to jail, Jesús. They'll say we killed the dog."

"Calm down. That's not going to happen."

"How do you know? Who are you calling?"

"The clinic."

Jesús spoke with the on-call vet who confirmed that Thor had already been cremated. When Jesús hung up, he was shaking.

The following morning, there was a SEBIN patrol car parked across the street from their house. Jesús went out, walked to the pharmacy on the corner, and from there he watched them for fifteen minutes. Then he went back home, without ever turning his head to look, and told Mariela what was going on.

"It's mad. I swear I don't get it."

Soon afterwards, the doorbell rang.

"It's them," said Jesús, checking through the window.

They walked out together to the gate that opened onto the street.

"Good morning," said Jesús.

"Good morning," said one of the officers. "I'm sorry to trouble you, but would you be so kind as to offer us a little coffee?"

Jesús and Mariela looked at each other for a second, totally unsettled.

"Sure," said Jesús, "of course."

"D'you want to come in?" added Mariela in a tiny voice.

"No need, señora. Also, the neighbors might think we're entering your house without a warrant. And that's illegal."

"Of course," said Mariela. "I'll go make the coffee."

And she went into the house.

She returned with three cups of coffee and handed them to the policemen and her husband. Jesús was talking to the officers.

"This is good coffee. Not like that overpriced crap they sell in the shops these days. Where d'you get it?"

"It's from some artisan producers. People from Trujillo. If you want, I can look for their card," said Jesús.

The policemen didn't answer. They were enjoying their last sips of coffee.

"Thanks."

They put the cups onto the tray that Mariela was holding and got back into their car.

"What were you talking about?" asked Mariela once they were back in the kitchen.

"About the state of things."

"Are you serious, Jesús? What if they were testing you? Or recording it?"

"My love, they're as fed up as we are. I'll bet that's the first decent coffee they've had in months."

They relaxed a little and spent the rest of the day at home, looking after the dogs in the small back garden they'd turned into a temporary shelter.

In the early hours of the morning, they heard banging on the front door, followed by barks and howls. The dogs in the back garden started barking. Jesús looked out the second-floor window and saw the same officers from the previous morning, barking, howling, and laughing. They looked drunk. There were lights on in the neighboring houses. It was then, with great effort, that the policemen jumped over the fence to the street and staggered back to their car.

Jesús and Mariela couldn't get back to sleep. At seven o'clock, they looked out the front again. The police car was gone. The old man next door, in his dressing gown and slippers, with deep bags under his eyes, said hi with a grimace.

"Such assholes," he said.

Jesús and Mariela kept watch over the street for a while.

"And all of this because of a dog, Señor Saturnino," said Mariela at last. "Honestly, I don't get it."

"It's not because of the dog," said their neighbor. "They do it because they find it amusing. They do it because they can. That's why. I'm going to try to sleep for a bit. God bless you."

A SEBIN car with different officers parked on their street every other day for the rest of that week. Jesús and Mariela couldn't sleep at night, waiting for them to raid the house or come in drunk and wreck everything. Mariela was on the verge of a nervous breakdown when they got the call from General Ayala.

Jesús insisted they shouldn't go.

"If he wants to help the foundation, he can put some money in the account. Or he can buy ten bags of food, but I don't see why we've got to go to his house."

They were intimidated by how far the house was, its impenetrable brick façade, with an electric gate, security cameras, and high-tension cables surrounding it, like a bunker.

Resigning themselves, like little calves on their way to the slaughterhouse, they rang the doorbell.

They were met by an old man in dressing gown and slippers, the way they used to see their neighbor in the mornings. Except that, compared to Señor Saturnino, this man who opened the door was kitted out much more elegantly. His eyes, somewhere between blue and green, made you lower your gaze. It was a nice feeling, like closing your eyes in front of a pond.

"I'm General Martín Ayala Ayala. Thank you very much for coming. Let's take this stone path. I want to show you the garden so you can meet the dogs. I've told them about you."

10

Jesús and Mariela never knew whether General Ayala had anything to do with it, but the fact was, after their visit to his house and telling him about the ordeal they were going through, the police didn't bother them again.

They met the general three or four times that summer, always at the same table overlooking the garden, where they shared coffee, orange juice, and some exquisite cookies. When Ulises Kan received the commission from the lawyer and called them for a first work meeting at Los Argonautas, that was also their chance finally to have a look around the place. The house, as they had already guessed, was huge. The space wasn't the problem, but the layout. It didn't seem to be the result of any design, but rather an architecture that had evolved by impulses.

The lawyer had given Jesús and Mariela a dossier with documents about the foundation. They were mainly instructions or practical advice. Like Ulises, they had received a copy of some plans proposing the optimal use of space. The general understood that the original project was likely to be partly altered, due to "the imponderables that always arise," as he put it in the letter accompanying the dossier, but hoped it would be followed as faithfully as possible. That was Ulises' role. To make sure everything was done correctly. They, meanwhile, had an additional assignment apart from the direct management of the foundation: to adopt Michael, Sonny, and Fredo as if they were their own dogs. Which meant that the couple had to relocate the dogs living in their El Paraíso house to Los Argonautas.

"The general was very fond of you. He said you were the son he never had," Jesús told Ulises.

"Really?" said Ulises. "I guess that's fair. He was the father I never had. But Martín was actually my father-in-law, and he did have two children. Paulina, my ex-wife, threatened to contest the will. They want the house."

Jesús opened his eyes wide.

"And what does that mean?"

"Oh, not much, really. They want to make it look like Martín was senile and that the will is invalid."

"But that's a lie," said Mariela.

"Of course it's a lie. I'm just telling you so you're aware of it. It's essential that we have good communication from the start, understood?"

They both nodded.

Where did that authoritativeness come from? Perhaps from the lingering air of disaster. It made him feel energized. Maybe the whole thing was an effect of the letter Martín had left him:

Dear Ulisito,

The Apocalypse is nigh. Sadly, I won't be here to see it. It's your task to build the ark and put your woman and your animals there and hold out for 40 days. Après le deluge, you need to wait for the dove with the olive branch. And once you have the branch, leave. There is no secret. The ark is the house. The strategic point to place it is on top of the mountain you spotted that first day. How to carry a house as big as Los Argonautas to the top of a mountain? That's the type of question I ask myself too, when I feel like a snail. Then I shout Mesopotamia, Tigris, Euphrates and they get disappointed in me. But I'm twice as disappointed in myself. Believe me. Only an orphan can understand the word of a madman. Take care, kiddo.

Love,
Martín

Nadine stayed behind, playing with the dogs. The echo of her laughter and the barking reached them across that labyrinth of oversized, ill-designed rooms.

They arrived at a kind of basement with three washing machines, two tumble dryers, two washtubs, and several ironing boards. Natural light lit the space, which resembled an army laundry. The light came from the garden, which it was possible to make out behind the white railings. Ulises found a set of keys hanging from a nail. He tried them one by one until he found the key that opened the gate. They stepped outside and stumbled upon a half-hidden plot of ground.

"The dog cemetery," said Mariela.

"Have you already been?" asked Ulises.

"No," said Mariela, "but the general mentioned it in his letter."

They walked around the graves of the four dogs in silence. Then they opened a low gate, hidden in the bushes, and came into the main garden. Nadine was surprised to see them, and the dogs ran over.

Nadine, Martín, jardín, thought Ulises.

Jesús and Mariela stayed with the dogs a little longer, while Ulises and Nadine sat at the table where the trainer and the vet used to meet the general to plan the setting up of the foundation.

"I need to read the letter he left them," said Ulises. "But I don't know how to ask for it without sounding suspicious."

"Why not just be frank? Show them your letter, too."

"I can't. If for any reason that letter ends up in Paulina's hands, that'd be the end of it all. They'd have proof their dad was crazy."

"But you know he wasn't crazy."

"Of course. But just me knowing that, it's not enough. The old man already knew how his children would come for me, and he wanted to warn me."

"He knew them well, then."

"At least he did Paulina. The lawyer's told me she's filed an appeal to get the will annulled. He didn't mention her brother."

"I told you I didn't like that family."

"Are your siblings like that?"

"One sister is a saint. My brother, an idiot. And then there's the twins, the older ones, who are psychopaths."

"And your parents?"

"They were sick, they mistreated us, but they didn't deserve to be killed."

"They killed them?"

"Yes."

"Who, the twins?"

"Yes."

"The Menéndez brothers?"

"Bingo! You've won yourself a first-class blowjob when we get home."

Until then, Nadine had always refused to talk about her

family. Ulises always tried to guess, but she'd start making things up. She'd come up with grotesque stories, making references to famous crimes, through which it was possible to glimpse scraps or threads of the original monster.

Mariela and Jesús came over. They locked the internal garden gate and sat at the table. Señor Segovia brought them a tray with coffee, orange juice, and the usual cookies.

"And what's this?" asked Mariela.

"Instructions from above," said Segovia pointing at the sky.

"I believe you," said Jesús. "The general calling us really was a miracle."

"We were about to get everything ready to run away," said Mariela.

"Where were you planning to go?" asked Nadine.

"To Lima. I'm from Peru," said Mariela. "My parents brought me when I was five. They're back there already."

"They say in the eighties, inflation in Peru was worse than we have here now. Is that true?" asked Ulises.

"Yeah, you'd go into a restaurant and the prices would practically go up between when you sat down and when you asked for the check."

"When I saw what they did to that little dog, the one they shot in the face, I remembered the things they used to say about the Shining Path," said Ulises.

"What did they use to say?" asked Nadine.

"When they wanted to announce their arrival someplace, in a village, for example, they used to hang the dogs from lampposts."

"How awful," said Nadine. "Is that true?"

"Oh, yes," said Mariela.

"I hope we never get to that point."

"Oh, I don't know," said Mariela. "The Shining Path were terrorists. And there was a war. And between the Shining Path and the soldiers, they committed all sort of atrocities. Here, on the other hand, it does feel like there's a war, only you can't see it. And it's the displaced, it's the people themselves, who abandon their dogs. That's worse than hanging them from a post. They abandon them to announce that they're leaving this hell."

11

General Ayala left specific instructions on where to set up: the clinic; the food, cleaning, and medical storage facilities; the administrative and accounting offices; Jesús and Mariela's permanent bedroom; and many details more. Despite all this, the description of the project still did not account for all the available space at Los Argonautas. The one thing General Ayala didn't leave a single word about was the garden. Should they install the dog kennels inside the house or in the garden? If the garden, they would need to build a roof. Should they use all the land or just part of it? And what would happen to Sonny, Fredo, and Michael if they used the whole garden?

"It's absurd Martín forgot about this specific thing," said Ulises. "Maybe the old man wasn't all there toward the end. I barely saw him during the last month. Shall I ask Segovia?"

Nadine set aside the thick white tome she was browsing and looked at Ulises tiredly.

"Come on, take off my panties."

Ulises knew what was coming next. Nadine asking him, or rather ordering him, to start sniffing and licking her. Ulises would do what Nadine asked and he would go astray shortly after. First the smell, then the taste, and then the divine mixture that soaked his whole face. Nadine trembling, grunting, sometimes screaming. Him becoming a lifeless body over which Nadine rubbed herself nonstop. Afterward, Nadine would be left exhausted and she'd sleep for three or four hours. Ulises would emerge from that frenzy, which left him completely awake, with gelatinous patches on his skin that dried off while he spent the afternoon lying in the hammock beside the apartment's huge balcony. Then, in the early morning, or the next day, Nadine's hand would search inside his underwear, waking him, so she could ride him or make him penetrate her. All with a furtive desperation that had little to do with hunger, passion, or love. But how could one know? What if love really was that total helplessness? Had anyone ever given him so much pleasure? And as for her, didn't she seem to be so full that she would sometimes weep with joy? Is joy what that was? He remembered his own tears in the dream about Claudia Cardinale. Where had they come from, anyway? Maybe he was the problem. Maybe, after all, he was still the problem. How could he love someone, or let someone love him, if he didn't know how to get the measure of his own tears?

This time, Nadine only slept for an hour and woke with a strange energy, one that could only be placated with a thousand-page book. As she browsed the thick white tome, she'd taken no notice of the printed pages, only the handwritten parts, where paragraphs were underscored, comments or doodles added around the edges. Some corners were folded down, not to mark any particular passage, but for the pleasure of drawing them as dog-ears.

"Look how cute," Nadine showed him, coming toward the balcony with the volume of the complete works of Elizabeth von Arnim.

"Yeah, it's cute," said Ulises, who always looked at her warily after those marathons of burrowing and friction.

"You don't get it. When you fold the corner of a page in a book, it's called 'dog-earing' it. And Altagracia used to fold them just to draw them. Supercute, see?"

Why that accent? Maybe it was normal after living in Buenos Aires for four years. Still, he didn't like it. Not the Argentinian accent itself, but her tone of voice.

"How do you know it was her?"

"You think Martín would have done these doodles? The handwriting reminds me of my mamá's. Also, Martín told me Señora Altagracia was a translator."

"What did she translate?"

"Legal proceedings, documents, that kind of stuff. From English."

Nadine kissed him and went to the bedroom to keep reading.

Ulises imagined Martín talking to Nadine about Altagracia. With a strong voice, albeit a little broken now, telling her who-knows-what anecdotes, under the almost unbearable light of his perfect eyes that forced you to look sidelong. And to hear sidelong, too.

That was the other side of General Ayala's inheritance, thought Ulises. A different secret for everyone.

He took a short nap in the hammock next to the balcony. Then he went to the bathroom and had a shower. He started to get dressed in the bedroom. Nadine was wearing one of his T-shirts and reading.

"How is it?" asked Ulises.

Nadine laid the book on her chest.

"Amazing. I'm reading her first novel, called *Elizabeth and Her German Garden*."

"Cool. Tell me about it later."

"Where are you going?"

"To talk to Segovia."

"Isn't it late?"

"A bit, but I really need to sort out this garden thing."

"This book can help you."

Ulises finished tying his shoelaces, went back into the bathroom, picked up his toothbrush, and applied some toothpaste. He stood in the doorway, brushing his teeth.

"It was her most successful book, and the most controversial, and her first. She wrote it under the name of 'Elizabeth.' It's the story of a woman who wanted nothing in life but to be left alone in her garden."

Ulises spat the foam into the sink and asked:

"Is that it?"

"She wrote some outrageous things. Well, things that must've been outrageous at the time. She calls the husband character 'The Man of Wrath.' And refers to her daughters just by the months of their birth: the March baby, the April baby, and the June baby."

"Not an exemplary mother, then," said Ulises, coming out of the bathroom.

"Not an idiot, more like. She wrote the book to pay her husband's debts. The book went through twenty editions within the first year."

"And what else?"

"I've only just started it, but I think there's a secret. And it has to do with the garden."

"It's a mystery novel, then."

"I'm not even sure it's a novel. It's more like a diary. The diary of a woman who, if she could, would have kept just one daughter, whichever, and the dog, isolated from the world, in her garden."

"Sounds kind of boring."

"It is. She goes into a load of detail about her routines for several pages. The little flowers she plants, silly arguments with the gardener, the type of seeds that work, and which don't. The social commitments, which she hates. I was about to give up reading until I realized that's just what Elizabeth wants: for you to get bored and close the book, so that she can be alone in her garden."

Ulises thought about his father-in-law. About his strange relationship with his wife, Altagracia. About the garden. And now Nadine. "I know you've got your own Claudia Cardinale, too," he'd said to him that time. Nadine, Martín, jardín, thought Ulises, positioning each of the words as if they were the corners of a triangle.

Nadine set the book down. Then she removed her panties and started touching herself.

"Come," she said.

12

Ulises had asked Señor Segovia to walk to the garden with him and share his thoughts about where best to install the kennels.

"Would you believe it, it's the only thing Martín didn't specify," said Ulises.

"This is Señora Altagracia's garden, she's the one who filled it with grass and flowers," said Segovia by way of explanation.

It was only then that Ulises really noticed Señor Segovia. Until that moment, with his solid and sober presence, he had been a friendly shadow.

"Excuse me asking, Segovia, but how old are you?"

Segovia let out an elderly guffaw.

Laughing like a tree, thought Ulises.

"Eighty-nine, Señor Ulises," he answered, and involuntarily rearranged his shirtsleeve, which covered a beaded bracelet.

"That's impossible. You're saying you're older than Martín . . ."

"That's right. But I'm the youngest. Francisco, my older brother, he's over a hundred."

"You're fucking with me, Segovia. That's impossible. And why are you still working?"

"If I stop working, I die. Same goes for my brother."

"The one who's a hundred? And what does he do?"

"Paco takes care of the Hotel Humboldt."

Ulises looked at the mountain. He cast his eyes over the outline of the Ávila range, searching in the distance for the shape of the Hotel Humboldt, standing like a space rocket over the bare summit.

"And how long has he been working there?"

"Since they built the hotel, in Pérez Jiménez's time."

"That can't be true, Segovia. You two must have made a pact with the devil."

"Or against the devil," answered Segovia.

"So it was your brother who sent the wreath for Martín's funeral."

"That's right, señor. They met in the times of the dog breeders, up there."

"At the hotel?"

"Nearby, close to the village of Galipán."

"I didn't know they bred dogs there."

"Not anymore. It was one of those ideas of President Chávez, who wanted to have a breeding center there for Mucuchíes—like Nevado, you know, El Libertador's dog. But it didn't work out."

Señor Segovia scratched his head.

"What happened?" asked Ulises.

Señor Segovia's laugh this time was sad yet mischievous, and he started walking to his bedroom.

Unsure whether he was invited or not, Ulises followed him.

The room was in the west wing, like a checkpoint halfway down the long corridor that went from the parking area, at the front of the house, to the laundry, at the back, where the garden started.

It was a small space full to the brim with boxes, suitcases, and general-interest magazines. Apart from that, there was only room for a bed, a rocking chair, and huge closet. Next to the bed, a bedside table with a lamp illuminating a radio that Segovia kept always on, and from which unspooled an endless rosary of boleros.

Segovia pointed at the chair, and he lay down on the bed.

The brothers Francisco and Facundo Segovia were born in La Coruña in the early twentieth century. Francisco in 1913 or 1915, a year before or after the war in Europe was declared. Facundo couldn't be sure. He did remember that his brother arrived in Venezuela in 1956, because he still had the postcard he'd sent him from the "Land of Grace," inviting Facundo to join him. Shortly after landing, Paco got a construction job on the Hotel Humboldt, the architectural jewel with which the dictator Marcos Pérez Jiménez wanted to crown his "New National Ideal" project. The New Ideal's main goal was, in Pérez Jiménez's words, "To win Venezuela a position of honor among nations and make a homeland that is more prosperous, more dignified and stronger every day." The government announced that the construction of the hotel would be completed in a record time of 200 days. In the end, it was done in 199. The most luxurious and exotic hotel in Venezuela, standing atop the Ávila, the mountain range above northern Caracas, opened in December 1956, and Paco has worked there ever since.

"He turned his hand to anything: he was a plumber, an electrician, a gardener, a watchman. Anything," said Segovia. He held out his arm and asked Ulises to pass him a worn-out folder full of papers.

Ulises did as he was asked and the old man searched for a while until he found what he was looking for.

"Here's a story they did on him for the *Todo en Domingo* magazine. Paco's famous!" he said, laughing.

The hotel was conceived for the exclusive use of the military top brass and the Caracas oligarchs. Because of its position on top of the mountain, you got there by cable car, and because the city's cable car had been out of service for many long years and at various other periods, the hotel had also been isolated during those times. That led to many stories of ghosts and hauntings that bound the glory years to those of neglect and decline. In the article, Paco reminisced about some of these chilling anecdotes, which put Ulises in mind of Kubrick's *The Shining*.

In the 1980s, during one of the longest periods the cable car was out of service, when the few tourists who made it to the hotel did so in the jeeps that could handle the steep mountain slopes, Paco received a gift: two Mucuchíes dogs. A male and a female. They were given to him by the retired general José Emilio Pinzón, as payment for some service that Paco never wanted to disclose. Not even to his brother.

"I learned about these things much later. I came to Los Argonautas after the death of Señora Altagracia. Around that time, I'd been forced to retire from my job as a guard at the Museo de Bellas Artes, and Paco recommended me to Señor Martín."

General Pinzón, Segovia went on, had just sold a farm in the Rubio region, in the state of Táchira. The guerrillas had kidnapped a cousin of his who worked there as a foreman, and he'd had to pay a fortune for his rescue. He had the two dogs at the property; they were about five or six years old. He needed to find them a home with a similar climate to the Andes.

"That breed really suffers in the heat, and they deteriorate," said Segovia.

And the only place in Caracas you find that climate is high

in the Ávila mountains, between the Hotel Humboldt and the small village of Galipán.

"Now, you might wonder why Pinzón didn't just leave the dogs in the same farm, or at a neighbor's," said Segovia, shooting Ulises a mischievous glance.

Ulises hadn't wondered anything, really, but Segovia wanted to tell his story. And after all, he asked himself, isn't that what a book is? A tree that wants to talk?

"This is the heart of the matter, Señor Ulises. When the general gave my brother the dogs, he advised him always to keep the male offspring, since that particular male Mucuchíes was a descendant of the first Nevado, El Libertador's dog."

At this point, Segovia's speech became a gurgling accompanied by gesticulating hands, which he would suddenly raise and then set back onto his chest, interlinked. Ulises tried to follow this absurd story about El Libertador's dog.

The old man's mind must be a bit gone, he thought.

Segovia mentioned a collar, a bloodstain, General Pinzón, and Chávez. A new vigorous whirl of words arrived, and then suddenly silence. Five seconds of silence that fell like a theatre curtain, and then the snoring of a bear.

Ulises stood up, trying not to make any noise, and left the room.

13

Ulises found Mariela and Jesús in the kitchen sitting in front of a laptop.

"What's up?" he asked.

"We're checking prices for dog food," said Jesús.

"OK."

"We'd need to look for it abroad. We've got to stop buying it from the only distributor left."

They'd just learned that three out of the nine dogs they had at their house in El Paraíso had suddenly died.

"Poisoned. We got a call from one of the shelters where we took the dogs when we moved in here. They say it might have been the food. Apparently, it was adulterated. Or maybe past its sell-by date."

Along with the dogs, they'd handed over the last sacks of food they kept in their house. They had bought them from a new distributor, since their usual one had left the country.

Señora Carmen interrupted them.

"Señor Ulises, there's someone at the door asking for you. A soldier."

"What do you mean a soldier?"

"A corporal, I think. Actually, he asked after Dr. Aponte."

Ulises went to the front door and found the young soldier. "M. Rodríguez" read the name sewn in black thread on one of the upper pockets of his olive-green uniform.

"How can I help?" asked Ulises.

"Is Dr. Aponte around?" said the soldier.

His brow was sweaty, and he turned every so often to glance at a jeep in the colors and insignia of the Bolivarian National Guard.

"Who told you to look for him here?"

"The doctor himself. He said to meet him here."

Ulises studied him for a few seconds. He was a boy. Eighteen, nineteen at most.

"Come on in, you can wait for him inside. We'll call him."

The soldier nodded straight away, with relief, but then the previous restless expression returned, and he didn't dare to move.

"What's wrong?"

He hesitated for a few seconds until, at last, he pointed at the car and said: "The dog. Shall I get it out the car? I just came to drop him off, really. I have to hurry back."

"What dog?"

The soldier wiped his sweaty brow with the back of his hand.

"Isn't this a vet's? Didn't Dr. Aponte tell you I was coming?"

"He didn't tell me anything. Just give me a moment. Wait here, I'll call him."

Ulises returned to the kitchen, where he had left his phone, and dialed Dr. Aponte's number.

Jesús, Mariela, and Señora Carmen followed the conversation in silence. When he had hung up, Mariela hurried to ask him:

"They brought us a dog? Where is it?"

Without waiting for an answer, she went to the door and the others followed.

"Where is it?" she asked the soldier.

The soldier pointed at the jeep.

They went around the car to the trunk, which was buttoned closed with the spare tire. The young soldier opened the door.

"Oh my god," said Mariela, stifling a cry.

Jesús was there in two strides. Señora Carmen steadied herself on the entrance gate. Ulises was still on the sidewalk, just a step away, motionless. He watched Mariela and Jesús carrying a gray blanket with a dying dog on it. As he went past, Jesús pushed him aside, not violently but with determination. There was no doubt about it, in their charge, the foundation would be in good hands. But what the hell was he doing there himself? As they went back into the house, Ulises understood, with pain and also with a bit of shame, that he was light years away from that transparent region where people like Jesús and Mariela lived.

"It's malnourished," said Jesús, kneeling beside the blanket, from out of which the animal's skinny nose emerged.

"These burns were made with cigarette butts," said Mariela angrily, standing up.

"It wasn't me. I swear it wasn't me. In fact, I'm getting in a lot of trouble even for bringing him out. That's why I called the doctor."

"How do you know him?" asked Ulises.

The boy mumbled: "I don't. The son, I mean. I know Dr. Aponte, the dad. From Fuerte Tiuna. He can explain everything. I got to get back to HQ before anyone notices."

His eyes were imploring, as if his life depended on his consent. Ulises nodded and the soldier left immediately.

"What did Aponte say?" asked Jesús.

"That we should take the dog in. That he'd explain later. We agreed to meet here tonight."

"We need to get him to a clinic," said Mariela.

"Not a clinic. I don't know why, Aponte insisted we don't take him to a clinic."

Jesús and Mariela exchanged a glance.

"Let's take him to our place then," said Mariela. "We've got what we need to look after him there."

"We'd need to spend the night there," said Jesús, looking at his watch.

"I'll fix some dinner to take with you," said Señora Carmen.

Ulises drove to El Paraíso, trying not to look in the rearview mirror at the little dog in Mariela's arms. Jesús sat in the passenger seat, silent. Ulises dropped them off, they said goodbye, and he drove back to Los Argonautas. He found Señor Segovia in the garden, taking measured steps across the grass and looking occasionally up into the sky, a sky where broken clouds appeared as evening fell.

"I've slept on it, and I think it's best to build the kennels inside the house," he told Ulises when he reached him.

"You think, Segovia?"

"Yes, better not to stir things up too much around here."

14

Señora Carmen had withdrawn early. By the time Dr. Aponte texted that he was outside, Segovia had long since retired to his magazine-crammed cave, with its lamp with the tiny bulb that spread an oily light, and the beat-up radio scattering boleros.

It was nine fifteen in the evening.

He didn't ring the doorbell, so the dogs didn't notice him either. On the short, paved stretch between the front door and the gate, Ulises felt sheltered by the house's protective darkness. Above him, a black sky with patches of clouds; below and in the background, the garden, like a calm sea. For those few seconds, as he opened the door and guided Dr. Aponte to the kitchen, Ulises felt like he owned something.

To share a house and a dog with Nadine. That's all I want, he thought. He checked his phone and saw he didn't have any messages from her. He hadn't texted her either. He hadn't had the time on that long day.

Once in the kitchen, which Señora Carmen had left immaculate, he realized he had nothing to offer to Dr. Aponte.

"Would you like some water? By the way, I only know your surname."

"Edgardo. My name's Edgardo. Haven't you got any whiskey?"

Dr. Aponte was a very large man. Tall, and of an obesity that was substantial but healthy. He looked exhausted.

"I'm not sure. There's bound to be some, somewhere," answered Ulises and went out to the pantry to see if he could find anything.

When he came back to the kitchen, Aponte was gone. Ulises heard his heavy footsteps in the living room, then one of the cabinet doors opening and closing, and again his steady footsteps on the parquet floor. He was carrying a bottle of Old Parr that looked tiny in his hand.

"Fetch some glasses. Let's go to the living room," he said.

Ulises obeyed. They made themselves comfortable in two large armchairs, then Aponte poured two fingers of liquor into each glass, and they toasted.

Ulises felt the brief euphoria that had come over him just moments earlier evaporating with the initial rush of the whiskey.

"A lot of work?" he asked Aponte.

"A lot. Same as usual. So, tell me, what did you do with the dog?"

"Jesús and Mariela took him to their house in El Paraíso."

"OK. They didn't go to a clinic?"

"No. They took him straight there."

"Great," said Aponte, now more relaxed, and he gave a rhino-like yawn.

"So what happened?"

Aponte took a second gulp and watched him, his eyes sharpening.

"The soldier didn't tell you?"

"No. He just said he knew your father. Something to do with Fuerte Tiuna, and that was it. He seemed scared."

"And with good reason."

Edgardo Aponte's father was also a lawyer. In fact, whenever Dr. Aponte's name was mentioned, people always understood it to be referring to the father, not him. He was a consultant to the Academia Militar. And just over a month ago he had taken on the defense of a general accused of conspiracy.

"Is it true he was conspiring?" asked Ulises.

"My father says no, but most likely yes."

"How'd you know?"

"Because everybody in there is conspiring, and they all get caught. That's how it goes. The thing is, there was a leak and they found out that General X—let's call him X—was up to something. The leak also leaked, so General X took his family off on a 'vacation.' As soon as he set foot outside the country, the government channel denounced the coup they were plotting. Now he can't come back. Problem is, General X couldn't take his dogs with him. He left them with the maid, since he was just going on a vacation, you see? And what do you think those sonofabitches did? They arrested the maid and took the dogs. The poor woman is over seventy and with a heart condition, so they had to let her go. They kept the dogs."

"How many dogs are there?"

"There were two. One's now dead. The other dog is the one they brought you."

"They killed him?"

"Yes. First, they starved him. Then they tortured him. They recorded everything and sent it to this general, who's also a dog nut."

"Unbelievable. How come the other one got saved?"

"My father went to the building in Fuerte Tiuna, the place the dogs were being held, because the general was pulling his hair out in despair when he saw what they were doing to his pets. No one came to meet him. So he waits for two hours and as he's walking back to the parking lot this guy comes over to him. He tells my father they killed one of the dogs, and offers to save the other one. That's when my father called me, and I asked the man to bring the dog here."

Aponte moved to serve Ulises some more.

"I'm good, thanks," said Ulises. "So what's happening now?"

Aponte poured a bit into his own glass.

"Let's just pray the young soldier didn't get caught. As for you, I don't know. When the little dog is recovered, he needs to be taken out of Caracas."

"This is so mad."

"It is, we're in the hands of madmen," said Aponte. He gulped down what was left in his glass and stood up. "I'm going."

Ulises stood up, too.

"No need to see me out. Thanks for the whiskey. We'll talk some other time about how things are going around here."

Ulises sat down. He looked around the living room, now empty, and once again had the impression that the place was his home. But it wasn't. His home was wherever Nadine was. He stood up again, turned off the lights and left. Before opening the gate to the parking area, he texted Nadine: *I'm exhausted. On my way. I love you!*

He drove through a dark, sleepy city, meeting few other cars. Entering his apartment, he found all the lights off. He turned on the one in the entrance hallway. He went to the kitchen and poured himself a glass of water. He walked into the bedroom carefully, so as not to wake her. As soon as he came through the doorway, he felt an absolute silence solidified into cold. He switched on the light. The cold was emanating from the double bed, larger than ever now, unmade and empty.

15

Nadine didn't return to the apartment that night or any of the nights that followed. Ulises was overcome with dejection. Her absence felt like a knife of air plunged into his chest. He postponed the definitive decision about the garden until her return, as he did sense that she would return.

Jesús and Mariela took the week off to look after General X's dog. They wanted him to stabilize a little before handing him over to a vet friend who would take him to Maracay. They also took the opportunity to clean the place and tidy up and to be seen by the neighbors. According to old Señor Saturnino from next door, a representative of the local Communal Council had been wandering around outside the property.

"I told them you were on a trip, but you were about to come back. If you aren't careful, those bastards will occupy the house and you'll never get them out."

Ulises told them not to worry. He would supervise the work that week. Martín had left contact details for Severo, a trusted builder who would be installing the new electrical system. Severo was no trouble. He just needed taking to hardware stores to buy materials, or to discuss the design plan and spec left by Martín. Normally, it was enough just to listen to him explain what he was going to do. Severo seemed to be a talkative man, but most of the time he was just thinking out loud. He was the type of person who needs an audience in order to sort out his own ideas.

Ulises spent the empty hours, which was most of them, wandering around the house, getting lost on that twisted path of empty rooms. Or in the garden, playing with the dogs for a while, watching the mountain in the park and soaring in his mind over the soothing rippling of the waters like a salmon. When he'd had enough of being in the garden, he would look for Segovia, but the man always seemed to be busy. And, sometimes, Ulises could swear that the old man disappeared entirely.

On those occasions, Ulises usually ended up in the library, sprawled over a comfy recliner, while looking at the Bolivarian gallery of illustrations on the walls. He would scan the dusty, blue-black tapestry of bound books. Which one would have the key to the secret passage? Which activated the revolving door when you pulled it out? He would stand up, moving his arm like a metal detector over the sand, and stop in front of a book. He would pull it out and then listened to the mechanism. At first, he thought it was the revolving door, but then he would freeze at the realization that the book was actually the firing pin of a giant revolver he had just set to open fire. But where was the trigger? Where?

Sometimes he managed to wake up by himself. Other times, it was Segovia who appeared out of nowhere and gave his shoulder a gentle shake. He would have the same nightmare in those short fifteen- or twenty-minute naps. These were strange days that led to a no less strange routine: writing in his notebook until he fell asleep. He would start with some bizarre title, like "The Knife in the Air," "The Trigger Book," or "The Sonorous Salmon," and that would lead him to weave words like the threads of a shroud for hours on end.

At least, that's what happened while Nadine wasn't around.

The only slightly interesting event happened in the middle of that week. During one of his library naps, Segovia woke him with the announcement that they had visitors.

"Who?" asked Ulises.

"The police."

He immediately cleared his head and went to the front door, where two men were waiting for him. One was in his fifties. He wore a black jacket, a white shirt, jeans, and loafers without socks. His hands were in his pants pockets, and he seemed absentminded. The other man, younger, did actually look like a policeman.

"Miguel Ardiles, forensic psychiatrist," said the older man, holding out his hand. "And this is Officer Reyes, posted here from the Chacao Police."

Ulises could smell alcohol.

"We have a court warrant to conduct a brief inspection of the house. Señora Paulina Ayala has requested a psychological autopsy of her father, General Ayala, as part of the trial for contesting his will. I imagine you've been notified."

Ulises invited them in. Officer Reyes, however, just handed him the paper with the warrant and said goodbye.

As they walked in, Ulises asked Ardiles:

"What exactly is a psychological autopsy?"

Answering this question was among the most boring parts of Miguel Ardiles's job.

"In order to contest the will, your wife needs to prove that General Martín was mentally incapacitated at the time the document was written."

"Ex-wife," said Ulises.

"I beg your pardon?"

The smell of alcohol on his breath was now undeniable.

"Paulina is my ex-wife. We are separating, as you can imagine."

"Of course. Can I tell you something without offending you?"

"Let's see."

"I can't stand that woman."

Ulises smiled and said:

"Fancy a whiskey, Dr. Ardiles? So you can tell me more about this, because I don't know much."

"Of course. Just Miguel is fine, if you like."

"Certainly."

He led him to the library. Miguel Ardiles looked at the illustrations and the portraits of Simón Bolívar as if he were in a dream.

Ulises let him have the recliner and found himself a hard wooden chair.

"Segovia, may we trouble you for a little whiskey?"

"I'll fetch it for you. Does the gentleman prefer water or soda?" Segovia asked the psychiatrist.

"Water, please."

When his first whiskey had been poured, Ardiles got straight to the point.

"Look, Ulises, I'll tell you how it is. My function here is to write a report saying Señor Martín Ayala was stark raving mad and therefore the will is invalid."

"And what would you base your assertion on?"

"On the family's testimonies and on the inspection I'm carrying out right now. Everybody knows Señor Ayala had a psychotic episode after the death of his wife, Señora Altagracia. I had to treat him then, didn't you know that?"

"Not really, no," Ulises admitted.

"Well, now you do. He was hospitalized for a while, then he came back to this house. That's when he started telling everybody to fuck off. He also started his habit of picking dogs up off the street and burying them in the garden. I don't know what happened after that. By the way, you need to show me the cemetery to take some pictures. I've always wanted to see it."

"No problem."

"There's something else. Apart from 'exhuming' the General Ayala's mental capacity in his later years, I need to show that this condition placed him in an adverse situation, ideal for opportunists like you who only want to take the old man's money and property. It's nothing personal, Ulises. We all do whatever we need to do to survive in this shithole. Do you follow me?"

"Absolutely, Miguel. What I don't get is why you're telling me all this."

"Because I like you," said Ardiles raising his glass a few centimeters. "In any case, my report is just part of the whole wider charade. The case is won by whoever has the best contacts upstairs. You or your wife."

"Ex-wife."

"Right. Ex-wife. Let's drink to that. Shall we have one more, then you can show me the dog cemetery?"

"We'll go in minute. What exactly did happen to Martín, if I may ask?"

Miguel Ardiles clinked his shot of whiskey and replied:

"The old man blamed himself for his wife's death. He told everyone he'd killed her."

16

When he had finally gotten rid of the psychiatrist, Ulises Kan returned to the library and lay back in the recliner. As he began to nod, he suddenly noticed the small table set against the wall. It was made of wood, semi-circular, and it stood on a single leg that looked like a billiard cue, thick at the top end, and tapering into the floor, a worn parquet of rotting slats. That was where he had taken the chair from, the one where he'd sat while the drunk psychiatrist talked to him about his inspection.

Ulises would get worked up on an everyday walk if he noticed a façade, or a bar, or an old advertisement he hadn't seen before. Whatever it was, no matter what, that had been right under his nose, day after day, unnoticed. That absurd table, for example. And it was obvious that he'd fallen asleep again, as he heard some footsteps and a lock opening, and he saw the semi-circular table rising from the floor. Not in a uniform, vertical movement toward the ceiling, as if levitating, but folding onto the wall. The leg had left the floor and was rising like a remote-controlled cannon. Then a square on the parquet floor opened like a submarine hatch, and he saw Señor Segovia.

The parquet floor surrounded his waist, as if he were in a swamp. From the hole where he stood, he dug up a medium-size box, which he placed on the floor, and then climbed the last rungs of the secret ladder connecting the library with the hideout. He shut the hatch, returned the table to its original position, and looked at him with his tree-like smile.

Now he'll wake me up, Ulises thought. But Segovia just pointed to the box and said:

"You'd better take it home with you, Señor Ulises. I'm afraid we'll be having more of these visits."

Ulises asked him to explain everything. The box, the hideout in the library from where he had spied on him, this business about the visits. But Segovia dismissed him with a wave that seemed to mean "later, later."

"Now, just take this home," he repeated. "I suppose you've already changed the lock at the apartment, right?"

"No."

"Then do it tomorrow. Do me that favor, too. I'll give you Señor Martín's contact. They're suppliers and they also have a lock installation service. Tell them you're General Ayala's son-in-law. But take this away at once."

Ulises carried the box to his car and drove back to his apartment. Nadine wasn't there. He phoned her that night, as he had on the previous ones, but she still didn't answer. He was afraid there might be a head inside the box. Altagracia's, for example.

But when he opened it, he didn't find much.

There was a very old photocopy, practically unreadable, of the manuscript of *El perro Nevado: Leyenda histórica* (1923) by Tulio Febres Cordero, in a see-through folder, which in turn was inside a manila folder held with worn rubber bands. Some love letters addressed to Altagracia. Other letters from former comrades in arms. He was drawn to two letters from some lawyer called Rodríguez, whom Martín had tasked with investigating the identity of his biological parents, a search that was apparently inconclusive. There was a second see-through folder with photos of Martín and Altagracia's wedding, and photos of Paulina and Paul as children. Ulises paused at one showing Martín holding two babies, on the back of which he had written: *My two little darlings, three months old each, so six in total.* Apart from that, the bulk of the box's contents was a huge, printed text, split into three bound volumes, entitled *Elizabeth von Arnim. Collected Works. Vol I. Vol II. Vol III. Translation: Altagracia Bautista.*

Nadine's going to like this, he thought. And he began browsing, passing the time, as if Nadine might return that evening. He knew she wouldn't, but he couldn't help but give in to some sort of waiting. In the end, that's what defines an orphan who has also been abandoned and put up for adoption: waiting. Waiting endlessly for the arrival of someone who's not going to arrive.

The next morning, Ulises called the contact Señor Segovia had given him. He had to choose two very expensive Mul-T-Locks, since those were the only locks they had.

"You have twenty minutes to complete the transfer," said the woman serving him. "After that time, we can't guarantee you'll get the locks, and refunds take five working days."

"OK," said Ulises, crossing his fingers that the internet connection didn't go down just then.

He was lucky and managed to complete the transaction. He called the locksmith back and gave the transfer number.

"Confirmed, Señor Kan."

"Great. What time can you come to install them? Like I said, it needs to be done today."

"I'll find out. Please stay on the line."

Ulises heard some noises in the background and then the same woman taking to someone else on the phone. He heard "Franklin," "Valle Arriba," "two Mul-T-Locks."

"The locksmith says he'll come by between midday and four or five in the afternoon. The installation is not included in the cost. Do you want to proceed?"

"Yes, please."

Ulises called Los Argonautas and spoke to Segovia.

"Segovia, I'm sorting out the locks for the apartment. I don't think I can get there today."

"That's fine, Señor Ulises."

"I need to ask you to deal with Severo today."

"No problem, Señor Ulises."

Ulises hung up. He was a bit disappointed by Segovia's servile tone, without even a hint of complicity. Didn't they share a secret now?

He lay in the hammock beside the balcony, from where he kept his eyes on the box, which he'd left in the middle of the living room like a small coffin awaiting its funeral procession. But was there a secret, really? He'd found nothing compromising among the things in the box. Mundane objects, traces of someone who had ceased to exist. Planets that remained in their orbits while holding a vigil for a dead sun.

He turned his gaze to the windows and was entranced to see such a beautiful sky, with its bright light. Caracas's perfect climate, the only immutable thing amid the hurricane. The climate and the Ávila mountain, he thought, which from this part of the city, on his Valle Arriba balcony, could be seen in all its splendor.

He reached for his cellphone and dialed Nadine's number.

He needed to listen to those beeps, which in his mind were the chimes from a postapocalyptic church marking the hour in a deserted town.

"Hello?" said a woman's voice.

"Hello, Nadine? Is Nadine there?"

"She's having a shower."

He noticed a slight foreign accent.

"I'm sorry, who am I talking to?"

"This is her mamá."

"Oh—well, pleased to meet you, señora. My name is Ulises. Could you ask her to return my call?"

The voice hesitated.

"Actually, she shouldn't know I've spoken with you, Señor Ulises."

"So you know who I am?"

"More or less."

"Has Nadine told you about me?"

"Look, I need to hang up. I'll call your number tomorrow, is that alright?" she said and then hung up.

The afternoon seemed to go on forever, while he waited for the locksmith. The man, in his sixties, arrived drenched in sweat.

"A lot of work today?" asked Ulises.

"Oh, not really, it's just that I came by foot."

"From Santa Fe?"

"And from Chacaíto before that. My car broke down a month ago. You can't get the parts. And public transit is impossible. What buses are left, are always full. Now they've got these trucks, kennels they call them, but I'm not getting into one of those."

The locksmith was very chatty, which was fortunate. It

helped him stop thinking about the phone conversation with Nadine's mother.

Despite its being two big locks, one for the front gate and one for the apartment door, the job was finished in less than an hour. However, the locksmith had to wait another hour for Ulises to transfer him the payment for the installation, because the bank website was down.

"What a mess," said Ulises.

"It's not that I don't trust you. It's just, because you and me have the same bank, I can access the funds straight away. And I want to make sure so that I can put down a deposit to reserve some shoes I saw near my house. Look at the state of these ones. They were new, and in less than a month they're already ruined."

Ulises saw the loose soles and crushed toes of the locksmith's shoes.

"A day will come when all this will be over," said Ulises. "Or when everything will stop and collapse, but we can't go on like this."

"Oh, I don't know. Sometimes I think things can get infinitely worse. I can't see a way out."

Ulises remembered what Mariela had told him. That no one gets out of here with clean hands. This particular hell had *lasciate ogni speranza* written not at the entrance, but at the exit.

"In order to get out, you've got to kill your dog first," Ulises translated, suddenly overcome by distress.

"Let's give it another go, Franklin," he said with a sigh, sitting in front of the computer. "Then I'll give you a lift to Chacaíto, how does that sound?"

"Thank you very much."

Ulises managed to make the payment at last. The locksmith gathered up his things and they set off. One of the most impressive changes Caracas had experienced with the crisis and general stampede is that there was hardly any traffic. They reached Chacaíto in minutes. In that short time, they saw three of those so-called "kennels." They were pickup trucks with bars attached to the back, with people piled up inside. Some were smiling. Others looked like sick animals.

Ulises slowed down a bit.

"Where do you live, Franklin?"

"On Panteón. Opposite the Biblioteca Nacional."

"I'll take you there, then."

"There's no need, Señor Ulises. Honestly."

Ulises took no notice and accelerated.

Soon afterward, he stopped at the door of a small house on a cul-de-sac parallel to the beginning of Panteón Avenue, near the Biblioteca Nacional.

"Again, thank you very much. That was very kind of you. It's little things like this, that's what helps you keep going. For one more day, at least."

The locksmith opened the car door, put one foot out onto the sidewalk and then stopped. He brought his foot back inside the car and locked the door.

"I almost forgot the most important thing," he said, and took two sets of keys from one of his jacket pockets. "I was just about to leave you locked out of your apartment," he laughed as he handed over the keys and got out.

Ulises travelled back along the Cota Mil, bordering the Ávila mountainside. He drove down Altamira, then through Plaza de Francia and took the Eastern Highway. He still had to face the night ahead of him, filled with questions, before he would be able to speak to Nadine's mother the next day.

Back at his apartment, it took him a couple of minutes to find the right keys. It felt strange to be inserting a new key into new locks that just led to the same old house. Segovia's worries about Paulina and her associates getting into the house had been dispelled. And now, he even thought it ridiculous, as their old life together seemed so far away that he was sure that nothing she could do would really affect him.

Could he say the same about Nadine?

Once inside, he searched for his notepad and started writing Nadine a long letter. Explaining to himself, through it, the meaninglessness of his own life. He stopped at three in the morning because he was tired. He looked for his cellphone before going to bed. He no longer expected her to answer, but he needed to hear the ringing, at least. That form of rejection was the only thing tying him to her, and without that solace, pathetic as it was, he wouldn't be able to sleep.

His finger hovered over Nadine's name for a few seconds and then, in a fit of rage, he got up and smashed the phone down on the floor.

17

The next day, Ulises woke up with a sort of moral hangover. He was going to need to write to Aponte to ask for a new phone. An iPhone, maybe. He'd always wanted one. Then he remembered that Nadine's mother was about to call and ran into the living room. He picked up the bits of cellphone scattered around the floor and rearranged them as best he could. The screen was cracked, and one side of the case was broken from the impact, but it seemed to work. More relaxed now, Ulises made breakfast.

He received the call around midday. The first thing Señora Kando said—that was her name—was that Nadine was on her way.

"Did Nadine say she was coming to my house?" asked Ulises.

"She didn't, but she had a bad night, and wasn't around in the morning."

"And how do you know she's coming here?"

"Because mothers know their children, Ulises."

She's figured it out, Ulises thought. He didn't have a mother or a father, and nor had he ever been a son himself. In situations like these, where he couldn't grasp life's instinctive codes, he felt like a robot, a replicant about to be subjected to the Voight-Kampff test.

"What's the matter with Nadine?" he asked.

"Firstly, she's not called Nadine. Her name is María Elena. And I'm her grandmother, really. But I raised her, because her mother lives in France."

"Is she French?" asked Ulises, as if pinning his hopes on that idea.

"Who?"

"Nadine's mother."

"No, she's Venezuelan. I'm the only foreigner, but from Montenegro, I was born there ages ago. What else did María Elena tell you, may I ask?"

Ulises told her what he knew about Nadine. Señora Kando listened to and denied and corrected each of his words. He assimilated everything that guttural voice told him, like an old sparring partner who's taken too many blows and doesn't feel anything anymore. That's how he learned that Nadine, or María Elena, wasn't a dancer either, nor had she lived in Buenos Aires for the last couple of years, but in Isla Margarita, with her husband and their child. Afterward they had moved to Caracas.

"She's a yoga teacher. She spent three months in India, in an ashram, but that was all. It was when she got back, though— that's when the troubles started."

"Nadine has a daughter?"

He remembered the scar on her belly, more solid than any book or any movie, and which he hadn't known how to interpret.

"Yes."

"How old?"

"Three. Almost four."

"And where is she?"

"Here, with me."

"And why isn't Nadine looking after her?"

"Before that, I'd need to tell you why María Elena's mother didn't look after her either. It's a long story."

"And the father?"

"That's what I wanted to tell you about, but first I needed to know who María Elena was with. You seem like a nice guy. That reassures me a little. María Elena's husband is a very tormented person. And she doesn't help matters either, if I'm honest. But not a bad person, deep down."

Ulises didn't know if this last comment referred to Nadine or to her husband.

"Are they still married?"

"Yes. And on occasions like these, I'd rather let the other person know. If I get the chance, I mean."

"Are you saying this isn't the first time it's happened?"

"No, it's not the first time. I'm truly sorry, Ulises, but sometimes I can't sleep for thinking about this. This whole story with María Elena is going to end badly. I know that for a fact. The least I can do is try to stop it being a tragedy for other people, too."

A couple of hours later, Nadine came into the apartment like someone just back from a well-earned vacation. The first thing she did was ask about the box. Ulises said Señor Segovia had given it to him for safekeeping.

"We had a very strange visit this week. A really weird guy. He'd had a bit too much to drink. Paulina's hired him to do a psychological autopsy on Martín."

"What's a psychological autopsy?" asked Nadine.

Ulises tried to repeat what Miguel Ardiles had told him, while wondering about the expression on her face when he finally called her by her real name, María Elena. But he just went on talking. He dwelled on a number of details he hadn't noticed until that very moment. Then he told her about his naps and the dreams in the recliner in the library, and the secret place where Segovia would hide, and the box, and Señora Altagracia's translations of Elizabeth von Arnim. He even told her about his notebook for the first time, although he didn't mention the long letter he had written to her. It sounded so interesting, everything that had happened in just a week, it all sounded so unusual and authentic, that Nadine couldn't help but look ashamed.

Nadine came back from the kitchen with a bottle of wine. She poured two glasses and handed one to Ulises, then took the other and lay down on the living room sofa. She seemed concentrated on the glass, as if the story was emanating from that small well of blood, and Ulises' words were some exquisite wine her ears were savoring. And the way Nadine listened was so lovely, she was so absorbed in imagining him doing all the things he was telling her that, for the first time in his life, Ulises looked at his own image and found it beautiful. So beautiful that he had the absurd desire to be Nadine, so that the perfect man he was in that second could possess her, and leave her exhausted and asleep in this bed that she never should have left for so many days and that she wouldn't leave ever again, since it was from there that the scent of her man emanated. A scent she ought to preserve, because if it faded, it would be like losing herself.

When they finished the bottle, they went to the bedroom. They kissed for a long time. Ulises ran his finger over the scar on her belly. Then he started caressing her. As he penetrated her, he repeated her name: Nadine, Nadine, Nadine.

Ulises finished soon afterwards and collapsed like a horse whose heart had exploded during his final race.

Nadine took his head and rested it on her chest. And began to whisper to him, until he fell asleep:

"I'm here. I'm here. I'm here."

18

He was woken by a call from Mariela. In a frightened voice, she told him there was a very suspicious car parked opposite the house.

"Since when?" asked Ulises. He realized he was alone in the bedroom.

"Segovia has checked the CCTV and the car came at dawn, around five."

"I'm on my way," said Ulises and he hung up.

He ran his hand over the other side of the bed. He was naked. He didn't like waking up like that, like a newborn. He put on a dressing gown and looked around the living room. The box was open. Nadine lay on the hammock, asleep. By her feet, on the floor, he saw the collected works of Elizabeth von Arnim and the three hefty volumes containing Señora Altagracia's translation.

He returned to the bedroom and finished dressing. Then he walked back into the living room, and over to the hammock.

She looks dead, he thought. The most beautiful dead woman in the world.

He bent over and kissed her forehead. Nadine took a deep breath, as if resurfacing from the depths, and opened her eyes.

"I'm going to Los Argonautas to take care of something."

"OK," said Nadine, stretching her arms and turning around. As Ulises put his key into the door, he heard her sleepy voice: "No one is to touch the garden."

The car, a black Toyota Corolla, had come up the cul-de-sac just minutes before five a.m. It appeared suddenly, piercing the black background and parking right opposite the house. Segovia had noticed it when he went outside to check the mailbox. He took out the two envelopes he found, then went straight to the small room between the kitchen and the pantry, the place from where he monitored the CCTV. After checking the recordings from the early morning, he asked Jesús and Mariela if they recognized the Toyota. It was eight o'clock now, and the car was still there. That was when they called Ulises. Minutes after the call, the driver started the car, turned it around and drove off.

"When did you get back?" Ulises asked them.

"Last night. We handed the dog over to our vet friend. They left Caracas yesterday," said Mariela.

They were convinced it was the police, wanting to scare them again because of the Thor case. Segovia, meanwhile, claimed that it was all to do with the girl Paulina.

"What shall we do?" asked Jesús.

"Let me go talk to the security guard," said Ulises.

He got into the car and drove to the guardhouse that controlled access to the development. The guard, a man as thin as parchment, didn't remember any car fitting that description coming in at that time. Ulises insisted that the security cameras had picked up a car like that, at that time, coming from the end, or rather the beginning, of the street.

"You must remember," Ulises insisted.

With great effort, the guard got to his feet and held himself upright in the doorway of the guardhouse.

"Are you drunk?" asked Ulises.

The man, who could have been his grandfather, shook his head no and began to wail:

"Hungry, that's what I am, señor. I've only been eating just a little rice in the morning the last three days. Several cars did come in and out last night. I just let them in and out. That's the truth. I couldn't stand up to see who they were. I'm sorry. I hope nothing bad happened."

Ulises felt a pang in his stomach. He'd left the apartment without having had breakfast, not even a coffee, and his stomach was already rumbling.

"No, it's me who's sorry. Wait for me here, I'll bring you some food."

He drove back to the house and asked Señora Carmen to fix two arepas with butter and cheese. When they were ready, he took an avocado and a banana from the fruit basket. He also poured some guava juice from the fridge into a plastic container and put everything in a bag. He drove the short stretch back to the guardhouse.

"God bless you," said the guard. He took the bag, sat down and, leaning back against the wall, he started to eat.

Ulises returned to the house.

"What can we do?" asked Jesús.

Ulises thought about it for a few seconds.

"We'll set some food aside for the guard whenever we can. It's a wonder he didn't pass out."

"It's happening a lot," said Señora Carmen. "People are fainting suddenly on the street."

"I mean about the car," said Jesús.

"We can't do anything at the moment, except stay vigilant. And get back to work," said Ulises.

Around midmorning, Severo arrived with an assistant. He had already installed the electric wiring and the power sockets, and now it was time to paint the house. The idea was to have everything ready before the equipment arrived. According to General Ayala's instructions, that would occupy nearly all the first floor, which was the space designated for the X-ray room, the operating room, and the cubicles for consultation.

Mariela and Jesús, for their part, made the list of medical supplies. They had also spoken to their colleagues in veterinary clinics who agreed to sell them some used machines. They only needed to repair them and get new spare parts.

"But we'll need to buy those abroad," said Mariela.

"Along with the sacks of food," added Jesús.

"Right. I'll sort that out today," promised Ulises, and he called the lawyer.

Aponte invited him for lunch the next day at the Bistró Libertador, a downtown restaurant whose opening ceremony a few years earlier had been attended by the mayor of Caracas himself. The place had a black-and-white checkerboard floor with a 1950s feel. Ulises found Aponte sitting at a table and talking on the phone. Seeing Ulises arrive, Aponte raised an arm, gesturing to him as if he were one of the waiters.

"Oh, you've never been here before? It's a place for the Chavistas. A lot of government bigwigs come here. What do you fancy?" Aponte gave the impression they were lifelong friends or business partners.

"So, why are we here, then?" Ulises wanted to know.

"I had a meeting nearby, at the Waldorf Hotel. Besides, the food is great. Order whatever you want."

Ulises looked over the menu.

"What do you recommend?"

"The beef. They bring it in from Argentina."

"You order for both of us."

Aponte ordered two rib eye steaks with an avocado, a heart of palm salad, and two shots of whiskey to toast.

"What are we celebrating?" asked Ulises.

"I've won a very important case. And seems like things are moving forward. Tell me the thing about the spare parts again, I didn't quite get it."

Aponte listened, while devouring the contents of a breadbasket with olive paste, then said:

"I don't see the point in buying spare parts from the United States. Let's buy the machines we need brand new, and that's that. Along with the dog food. Send me the shopping list as soon as you can. Today is October 31. Which means we have around eight weeks to go. We're halfway."

"And if we don't make it for some reason, what happens?"

"Your apartment goes to General Ayala's children."

"What about the house?"

"The house gets taken by the Bolivarian Society—not sure if you know them—so that the institution can have a new headquarters."

"And if that's the case, what do you stand to lose?"

Dr. Aponte smiled and wiped his mouth with the cloth napkin on his lap.

"I lose five years of an annual bonus, which would be handy for taking away the headaches I get from time to time."

Aponte was in a good mood.

"And what would stop you executing the will in our favor?"

"I don't execute the will. My father does, he's General Ayala's true executor. And my father would sell me out before letting the general down. They were like brothers. That's why I've been insisting that the time limits laid out in the document should be met."

"What did Paulina say to you? Did she hint at anything?"

"You mean, did she want to buy me off? Of course she did. From day one. I told her the same thing I'm telling you now. On this matter, my hands are tied."

The waiter brought the dishes. They sat in silence for a long time, savoring the meat.

"And how old is your father?"

"My father is eighty-one. Why?"

"Forgive me for asking you this. But if something unfortunate happened to your father, who would execute the will then?"

"Then it would go straight to the general's children. But the old man is as strong as an ox. He has the triglyceride levels of a boy, and he's completely lucid."

"I didn't mean it that way. I shouldn't say this about Paulina, she was my wife after all, but I wouldn't be surprised if she tried something."

Ulises told him about the black car with tinted windows that had been keeping watch on the house. Also the conversation with the forensic psychologist.

Aponte listened, while concentrating on the juicy piece of meat.

"Well, we can't know if that car has anything to do with Paulina. Please, do let me know if you find out anything else. In the meantime, we need to keep the work going. By the way, I saw your email. I've ordered your phone. It should arrive in a couple of weeks. I'll send it over to the house."

"Is it an iPhone?"

"Yeah. Silver-plated, latest model, like you said."

"Thank you," said Ulises.

Aponte ordered two more whiskeys.

"We're going to make it. No doubt about that." And he toasted again.

19

On her return, and with Señor Segovia's help, Nadine repositioned the table with coffee, orange juice, and the delicious cookies. She arranged it all next to the flowerbed. There she settled with the volume of Elizabeth von Arnim's complete works and the three manuscripts of Señora Altagracia's translations. She took notes as she read, armed with a pen and a highlighter. She read leaning back in the chair, feet on the table. Sonny, Michael, and Fredo lay around her all morning.

"She looks like a countess," said Mariela.

Jesús looked at his wife for a moment, then over at Nadine and said:

"Yes, totally, a countess."

Ulises let her be. After the meeting with Dr. Aponte, he dove into a vortex of work to try to finish setting up the foundation. His only rest during the day would come when he stopped every now and then to watch her reading, one hand holding the book and the other hanging down, distantly stroking the head of whichever lucky dog had gotten there first. Sometimes Nadine would look up, and while he carried equipment, desks, and boxes, she would give him a wave and keep on reading.

That same atmosphere would stretch out into their evenings

in the apartment. It was as if by talking so much about Elizabeth von Arnim and her two great passions, gardens and dogs, they had allowed her ghost to take over their spaces and habits. Ulises and Nadine, in some other dimension, had had five children, who one by one had left home. Which now made it possible for them to live there easily, without that stifling sense of duty.

Ulises talked excitedly about very mundane things, such as buying medical equipment, his conversations with Severo, who was fixing some leak, or the staff uniforms Mariela said she could procure.

"She says the foundation should have a logo. And it's true. Do you know any designers who could do the job?" asked Ulises.

And Nadine would say yes, or no, and straight away she'd start talking about Elizabeth von Arnim, whose real name was Mary Annette Beauchamp, and who was older cousin to Kathleen Beauchamp, who would follow her example and become a writer herself, adopting the *nom de plume* under which she would be known: Katherine Mansfield.

Nadine started with *Elizabeth and Her German Garden*, and *All the Dogs in My Life*. That is, Elizabeth von Arnim's first book, the novel published in 1898, and her peculiar memoirs, which came out in 1936, five years prior to her death. And now she wanted to read, in the chronological order in which they appeared, the other twenty novels von Arnim had written and published over that time. She had just finished *The Solitary Summer*, the one that followed the very successful *Elizabeth and Her German Garden*, which had sold out more than twenty editions in just a year and helped to make the society debut of a mysterious new writer who hid behind an all-too-simple pseudonym: "Elizabeth."

In *El verano de la soledad*, as Señora Altagracia had translated the title, the same Elizabeth from the first novel reappeared, alongside the now famous garden that its planter defended from the siege of visitors, from insufferable social engagements and even her own family—that husband and those children, whom she found an absolute hell.

That light-hearted treatment of the family, with its brutal honesty, had caused a scandal and quite a few problems for Mary Annette herself. Which explains that second novel's dedication: *To the man of wrath. With some apologies and much love.* That Man of Wrath was Count Henning von Arnim, who had been subtly ridiculed in Elizabeth's first novel. Until now, Nadine had only consulted Altagracia's translation whenever she wanted to clarify some confusing passage. As if the translation was a dictionary created to help understand this gigantic single volume of Elizabeth von Arnim's collected works.

Altagracia added multiple footnotes to the text. Some with details about the translation. Others, most of them, with facts about Elizabeth von Arnim's life. Others still with historical information about the Pomerania region or about the castle (which she called "the house") in whose garden the writer had found heaven on earth and where, for example, E. M. Forster, a close friend, edited the galleys of his first novel, *Where Angels Fear to Tread*.

The Solitary Summer ends with a rather disturbing scene. Elizabeth overlays the end of the story onto the end of the summer, since that is the plot: a woman decides to spend the summer at home, in her house with a garden, just by herself, with no visitors, to the amazement of her husband, who is certain that his wife will get bored and give up. However, the summer is now over, and despite some mishaps, Elizabeth thinks she has kept her promise and says as much to her husband, the Man of Wrath.

"If I remember rightly," he said, after a pause, "your chief reason for wishing to be solitary was that your soul might have time to grow. May I ask if it did?"

"Not a bit."

Count von Arnim is disarmed by the honesty of her answer and comes over to stand with his wife by the fire.

And, as usually happens, when tenderness has made him soft, he puts his guard up with a cheerful remark about honesty being a rare trait in women. Which unleashes one of the many scenes in which Elizabeth, angrily, rebukes her husband for his misogynistic views:

"You should be very happy and grateful to have a woman always with you."

"But am I not?" he asked, putting his arm around me and looking affectionate; and when people begin to look affectionate I, for one, cease to take further interest in them.

"And so the Man of Wrath and I fade away into dimness and muteness, my head resting on his shoulder, and his arm encircling my waist; and what could possibly be more proper, more praiseworthy, or more picturesque?"

"That's how it ends," said Nadine.

"It reminds me of the last scene of *Blue Velvet*, with the happy couple and the robin feeding the chicks," said Ulises.

"Now look at what Altagracia writes in her note: 'Elizabeth, you're always so witty, yet you lapse into this common banality believing all men to be the same. Just as your own husband thinks that of all women. All men are driven by wrath, but there are different kinds of wrath. Wrath can be gentle, like that of Count von Arnim. And wrath can be wrathful, if you like. Oh, Elizabeth, always so self-centered, you never experienced this last type. Lucky you.'"

"Weird, isn't it?" added Nadine.

"I thought Altagracia was fond of von Arnim."

"Of course she was. The whole garden thing was a way of being like her. For a moment, I thought Altagracia was referring to the circumstances surrounding Elizabeth's death. She's living in the South of France when the war breaks out and she flees to the United States. She dies in 1941, of old age, convinced, like Stefan Zweig, that Hitler would take over the world."

"Well, so that's it, then."

"I'm not sure. I was thinking about another possibility. That Altagracia wasn't really talking about Elizabeth, but rather about herself."

"About Martín, you mean?"

"Right. Martín as her Man of Wrath."

II.

20

"Gordo!" whispered Mariela. "Hey, Gordo!"

Jesús didn't move.

"Gordo, did you hear that?" repeated Mariela, shaking him this time.

"What is it? What is it?" said Jesús, half sitting up.

"Did you hear that?"

"Hear what?"

"The dogs were barking."

"Well, dogs bark. What time is it?"

Mariela checked her phone and the light from the screen lit up her face.

"Ten to four."

"Go back to sleep. We can still get a couple more hours."

Mariela got up and put on a dressing gown.

"What are you doing? Don't go outside."

"I'm just having a look."

Jesús lay down again, closing his eyes tightly.

"Gordo," his wife wasn't whispering anymore. "There's someone in the garden."

They looked out of the window in the hallway next to their second-floor bedroom. At the end of the garden, near the fence separating it from the Los Chorros Park, a shadow was stirring in the darkness. And in the shadow, a fuchsia glow.

"I can't see the dogs," said Mariela.

"I'm going down. You wait here."

"I'm coming with you."

The staircase led into the kitchen, then went on down to the laundry room. From there, they could only see part of the garden, since the cemetery was in the way, blocking the view, and the only light came from the lamppost that lit the street.

They heard the sound of legs, as if they were rubbing against each other, and once again, that fuchsia glow in the darkness.

It was Nadine.

"What's she doing?" whispered Mariela, standing on tiptoes.

"I think she's dancing," said Jesús, gesturing with his hand in a spinning motion.

The dogs were three obedient lumps, just sitting there, watching her dance. The glow in their eyes keeping time with Nadine.

They heard the wing flapping of her legs again, and this time they watched her landing from a short jump. One of her legs was slightly raised, held straight out, while the other, bent, carried her weight. Her arms were stretched out in a cross, like a ballerina completing a routine.

At that moment, Nadine's head turned 180 degrees, with the flexibility and accuracy of a dove, while maintaining her posture, and stared them both in the eye.

Mariela jumped and ran back upstairs. Jesús managed to stay just long enough to give her a wave and then he too hurried back up. As he walked into the bedroom, he found Mariela hiding under the sheets.

"What's the time?" asked Jesús.

Mariela looked at her phone.

"4:35."

"I'm going to take a shower. I'm drenched in sweat."

"Can I come to the bathroom with you?"

"Of course."

Jesús came out of the shower and Mariela got in.

"Stay here while I have a quick shower too," said Mariela.

Jesús finished drying himself, lowered the lid of the toilet, and sat down. When Mariela came out of the shower, they both dressed and waited in bed for the sun to rise.

Before they went down to the kitchen, Mariela asked her husband:

"What shall we do?"

"Tell Ulises, I guess."

In the kitchen, they found Señora Carmen finishing brewing the first coffee of the day.

"And Segovia? Is he still asleep?" asked Jesús.

Señora Carmen didn't answer. Instead, with the steaming cup in her hand and after taking her first sip, she pointed at the strange spectacle taking place outside the window. Down in the garden, dressed in a fuchsia leotard and a slim black T-shirt, Nadine was doing stretching exercises in front of the dogs.

"What's the girl doing?" she asked.

The three of them looked out the window.

"Yoga," said Mariela. "It's stretching exercises. That's the first pose. Sun Salutation."

Señora Carmen poured coffee into the other cups and handed them to Mariela and Jesús, and they carried on watching. Fredo, Michael, and Sonny were sitting opposite Nadine, closely following every one of her movements.

They finished their coffee. Señora Carmen looked at the bottom of her cup and said:

"I'll go see what's up with Segovia."

She left the kitchen, and while the shuffling of those tired feet was still audible, the dogs started barking. Mariela and Jesús looked at each other.

"You go," Mariela asked him.

Jesús found Nadine in the garden, sitting on the grass, her gaze, vacant, her fuchsia leotard a little muddy with dew-softened soil. When she recognized him, she just said:

"I didn't do anything."

That was when they heard Señora Carmen screaming.

Jesús ran to Segovia's bedroom. He pushed Señora Carmen aside and saw him lying on the floor. He wasn't asleep, nor was he snoring. The radio lay next to his body, wrecked and mute, like a forest cabin struck down by a fallen tree.

21

There were not many people at Señor Segovia's funeral. Mariela, Jesús, Señora Carmen, and Ulises from Los Argonautas. From his family, there was just Paco, his brother, who came with someone from the Caracas cable car company.

Nadine didn't want to go.

It had fallen to Ulises to call Señor Francisco and break the news. From the other end of the line came a string of sentences broken by the effort of breathing:

"Francisco Segovia, yes, señor. Facundito? Oh, God. My brother Facundito, that can't be true. Well, thank you for calling. No, there's no need to hold a wake. Yes, we have our plot in the Cementerio del Este."

They managed to arrange the funeral for the following afternoon. Though it wasn't a religious ceremony, Ulises felt he had to say some words. He highlighted Facundo Segovia's many years of work and loyalty in the service of General Ayala.

"And in recent months, with the whole big Simpatía por el Perro family."

He felt a bit ridiculous for using "whole big family" to refer to that small group of people. Mariela, though, seemed moved and couldn't stop crying. Ulises addressed his words to the old man. He kept his head down, listening. Perhaps thinking that such longevity had been a mistake, since who would go to his own funeral when he died?

Ulises finished his speech and the cemetery workers proceeded to lower the urn and seal the grave with fresh cement.

Paco Segovia followed the maneuver to the end with total concentration. Ulises came over slowly to say goodbye.

"Where are you off to now?" asked the old man suddenly.

"To the house. Why? Do you need a lift?"

"No, I'm going with Juancito," he said, motioning toward the man who had accompanied him. "Why don't you come with us?"

"Where?"

"To the cable car, where else?" he said, looking at him with eyes like sunken hazelnuts.

Ulises walked over to the group, exchanged a few words, gave Jesús his car key, and left with Señor Francisco.

They drove in silence from Cementerio del Este to Maripérez. Ulises thought it must be coming up for seven in the evening. He wondered how he'd get back home if the conversation dragged on very long.

They parked at the cable car lot and walked slowly to the station. The ticket windows were already closed but the mechanism would carry on working until eleven at night. That was the explanation they got from Juan, the driver, who hadn't opened his mouth until then.

"Evening, Paco," said the guard who escorted them to the ramp where the cabins came in and after a brief pause set off again. At that time of the day, they arrived loaded with people, did a short U-shaped loop, slowing and coming almost to a stop, re-emerging again reinvigorated, shooting back up toward the mountain, empty.

When it was their turn, Juan asked Ulises to hold one of Paco's arms, while he did the same with the other and the walking stick.

"Number three," said Juan.

They let two cars go by, and when the third approached, Paco himself announced:

"This is the one."

Juan got in first. Paco then gave a small leap and let go of Ulises, who had to hurry to get on last.

"Number three," said Paco smiling, already leaning back in his seat.

When they finally made it up the mountain to the north platform of the cable car, they found a crowd waiting for their turn to go down, after an afternoon of churros, strawberries and cream, ice skating, and that dose of biting cold you couldn't get anywhere else in Caracas. They moved against the tide, while the young people who worked the cable car cleared the path for them, following each other in turn with that watchword that would be repeated at the Hotel Humboldt facilities:

"Evening, Paco."

"What's up, Paco."

They climbed to the start of the paved path that led to the hotel.

"Wait for me here," said Juan.

After a while, Juan appeared at the wheel of a golf buggy. Paco took the passenger seat and Ulises went in the back. The journey took just a few minutes. The headlights set the pace, with their rhythm of lights and shadows. Some scattered couples and families were making their way back. Juan stopped the buggy in front of the terrace where the hotel building began, and they got out.

"Juan, take me in. You can look after the gentleman after-wards, while I rest for a while," said Paco without even looking at Ulises.

"No problem," said Juan. Then, addressing Ulises: "Wait for me here. I'll be right back."

"OK," said Ulises, not really understanding what was going on.

He watched them walk away toward the hotel entrance and down some side stairs. When he lost sight of them, he looked around and found himself alone. He looked at the mass that was the hotel. The first time he'd seen it, as a boy, on one of the few family walks he did with the Khans, he thought it looked like a rocket about to take off.

In that instant, he felt his skin crawl, and he understood that the night was an infinitely large cathedral. Hotel Humboldt was, at most, the mere splinter of a faraway prayer stool that he would never get to see. Or the residue of an incense stick dropped from a higher dimension to which this one, where he and everyone else lived, was nothing more than an ashtray. And amid that vastness, just when he felt himself no more than debris in the prodigious cycle of creation, the recognition from the pupil of an eye whose divine kindness was suddenly watching. Watching him. That worm. That forgotten parasite in the manure.

The feeling lasted mere seconds.

The noise of three golf carts, all loaded with drunken and noisy youths, burst the bubble. The effect created by the landscape and the late hour, ephemeral like a soap bubble in which colors and shapes from out of this world are sometimes reflected, vanished in the air.

22

The night of Señor Segovia's funeral, Mariela had a nightmare. She dreamed they were in their room in Los Argonautas and that they were woken by an earthquake. They ran out to the street. Everything was covered in ashes. Fire was coming out of the Ávila peak.

"A fire," said Jesús.

But Mariela could still feel the tremor.

"It's the volcano," she said.

Then, as if obeying an order, the lava began to erode the huge mountain as it hurtled downhill. It had already charred Cota Mil, which now resembled a huge, fossilized snake, and eaten away the front of the building at Los Argonautas. They needed to escape, but a horrific vision paralyzed them. Out there, behind the river of lava, with the mountain now erased, was the sea. And they would have burned to death there, if it hadn't been for Segovia, who came out of nowhere and broke the spell by telling them that to save themselves they only needed to board a boat on the peak of the mountain in the park, on the other side of the garden gate.

"The house is the boat," he said.

Mariela woke up in shock. Jesús stroked her hair, while she tried to convey the images she had seen.

"What do you think it means?"

"Nothing. It doesn't mean anything," said Jesús, drawing her close to his chest.

Something similar had happened in the dreams around the death of their daughter Amparito when she wasn't yet three years old. After that, they devoted themselves to saving street dogs, which was the only thing that could abate their anxiety.

Despite his reassuring tone, Jesús couldn't help but wonder the same thing. What could it mean? Why have this dream right after Segovia's death? What did God want to take away from them this time? This land really was cursed, if even the dogs could not be saved. They would need to leave Los Argonautas and the country, and take their compassion elsewhere.

Short barks interrupted the silence of the hour. Mariela and Jesús went straight out into the hallway. They looked through the window and scanned the darkness of the garden. Soon they spotted the fuchsia glow.

Mariela took Jesús by the hand, and they walked downstairs. Jesús was wearing the same old shorts he always slept in, and a t-shirt. Mariela, a thin dressing gown that barely covered the top half of her buttocks. The early-morning cold made them walk closer to each other, and faster. They positioned themselves in the same corner of the laundry room, this time making no effort to hide. Mariela standing in front of Jesús, leaning on his chest, his arms crossed around his wife's waist.

Nadine was moving backward and forward. Mariela and Jesús didn't know anything about dance or ballet, but there was something in the solemnity of her movements, in the hour and the audience she had chosen, that sent shivers down their spines but also moved them. Suddenly, Nadine seemed to fall to the ground and did not get back onto her feet right away.

The fuchsia stain stopped moving from the spot where it had fallen. However, the rubbing sound from the jumps and legs continued.

Mariela eased herself out of Jesús's embrace, searched for the key, and opened the gate to the garden. She walked across the dog cemetery and from there, protected by the hedge bounding it, watched what from the laundry room they had only been able partially to make out in blurry outline.

Nadine was naked. Her skin so white it gave her beautiful body a neon texture. When completing one of her movements she landed on her back and began to raise and lower her pelvis in a frenzy. Sonny stepped closer. Nadine kept moving, groaning and moaning ever more compulsively. Sonny reluctantly sniffed that nocturnal fruit and then walked away.

In the shadows, Mariela stretched out her hand until she found Jesús's cock, already wrestling with the fabric of his little shorts. She began to stroke him. Jesús took off his shorts and lowered Mariela's panties. He pulled her buttocks apart and penetrated her. He began to thrust from behind. Mariela grabbed Jesús's hand to cover her mouth.

Meanwhile, Nadine had stood up and begun to spin around again.

When they finished, they picked up their clothes and crept back to the house. Nadine wasn't dancing anymore. She was sitting at the table in the garden. She seemed to be holding an invisible pen in her left hand as if taking notes on a pad, which was also invisible.

23

Juan returned with a pair of flashlights. He handed one to Ulises and said:

"Come with me, I'll be the guide. I go first and you go last. You just need to keep quiet and make sure we don't lose any of these youngsters. Afterward, I'll take you to Paco's room so you can talk for as long as you want. Sound good?"

Ulises didn't have many options.

"Where are we going?" was the only thing he asked.

"To the hotel," said Juan, pointing at the building.

Then he switched on his flashlight and walked over to the group.

"Evening, folks. Are we all ready?"

"Yes!" they answered in unison.

No one was aged over twenty. Some girls were paired off with several of the boys. Those who were by themselves were noisier than the rest.

As they entered the building, they went down a flight of stairs, groped their way through some indecipherable rooms, and arrived at a sort of one-story house where the swimming pool was. The only light was filtered through the curtains from the floodlights outside, or came from their own flashlights.

Juan's was plotting their course, while Ulises' shyly swept away any shadows left by that fainthearted column who entered the hotel as if it was a jungle.

"Please be careful. I don't want anyone falling and breaking their legs, and me ending up losing my job."

The youngsters gave a nervous laugh and listened to the guide as he talked. Juan shared a few architectural facts, then recounted the legend of some young brothers who drowned in 1965.

"There are nights when you can hear splashing in the empty swimming pool. They say it's the children's souls."

There was an immediate wail of laughter and fear. The girls took refuge in their boyfriends' arms.

"We're going to the international hall now," said Juan. "Follow me."

It was like an Indigenous version of a house of horror. Only subtler and more chilling, as it needed merely darkness, the melancholy beauty of that architecture frozen in time, and the tales—partly made up, partly true—of what had happened in the hotel.

Juan repeated the same formula at every stop. He mixed historical facts with explanations about the architecture, name-dropping famous guests the youngsters had never heard of and ending with a tragic anecdote linked to some ghost or apparition.

On a couple of occasions, Juan added a postscript to his story that reinforced its verisimilitude and spurred the imagination:

"And if you don't believe me, you can ask Don Paco, who's been the keeper of the hotel for over sixty years."

After the international hall they went to the discotheque, then the kitchen, and they even had time to stop by the laundry and the machine rooms. It was a blue corridor that Juan pointed at, which would have been unremarkable had not Don Paco, that mythical keeper, suddenly appeared from one of its doors.

The kids gave a cry of alarm that made Paco turn around.

"Good evening, Don Paco. We're just finishing up over here," said Juan.

Paco waved them away impatiently and walked off, leaning on his walking stick, into the depths of the blue hallway.

"Believe it or not, Paco is 105. He came to the hotel in 1956 and has lived here ever since. Even in the years the hotel was closed to the public. You can imagine what those eyes have seen!"

Paco's sudden appearance turned Juan's mumbo jumbo into an absolute truth. Everything was set up for the last and most interesting part of the tour.

They returned to the main hall and began to climb the wide circular staircase.

"Where are we going?" asked one of the girls.

Juan stopped, held the flashlight under his face like the funny guy in a horror movie just before he gets killed with a chainsaw, and said with his most sinister smirk:

"To the twelfth floor. To the General's room."

They walked on and Ulises heard one of the boys quietly asking another:

"What general?"

To which the more knowledgeable one replied:

"General Pérez Jiménez, asshole."

"And who's that?" the first one insisted.

This time, the guy who seemed better informed hesitated.

"A dictator. The man who ordered all of this to be built."

Ulises' voice startled the back of the queue. The guys had almost forgotten he was there. Juan pointed his light at where he was for two seconds, before continuing their climb. They paused a few times to rest, looking through the sealed windows at the dark landscape as it turned gradually thicker.

Finally, Juan announced that they had arrived.

"This is the twelfth floor. General Marcos Pérez Jiménez used to stay in these rooms. Come on in," he said, opening the door next to him.

The young people walked fearfully into the room, taking such shorts steps that the group compacted, as if they were walking in a procession. The room was totally dark. Juan pointed his flashlight at the group.

"May I please come through?" he asked. His politeness made everything scarier.

The youngsters let him through, bumping into each other. Juan navigated between the bodies and reached the wall farthest from the bed. He pointed his flashlight and groped around the wall, and as soon as he had found the cord, he opened the blinds. A less oppressive night entered the room.

The group approached the window.

"That over there is the village of Galipán. And those two little lights in the background, the ones that look like a couple of low stars, they're really from a ship in the sea. There was a time when the cable car went all the way to Macuto, but that's not working any more. But it was the original plan. This country is beautiful. It's always been beautiful—on paper at least."

The evening's poetic moment, thought Ulises. No doubt about it, Juan was a master storyteller.

"As you can imagine," he added, "they held big parties at the hotel. There was one where a woman died. They say she was the General's mistress. They also say she made the mistake of sleeping with another man in the General's own room, and that he found them. We don't know whether the woman killed herself or got thrown out the window. Either way, the fact is that this is where she fell, from this very window."

Juan knocked at the large window as if it were a door and pointed the flashlight at some metal locks on the edges.

"See those? The window is sealed. There's no way of getting it open without breaking the locks. But sometimes it does just appear open. Naturally, people believe it's the woman's ghost, who wanders the twelfth floor. That's why almost nobody dares come up here. And if you don't believe me, you can ask Don Paco, who you already met. It's not something that anybody told him—he actually saw her falling. With his own eyes. And he also saw how the next day they tossed a body wrapped in a sheet down the other side of the mountain."

Nobody moved or said a word.

Juan looked at his watch and announced:

"Time to go down."

24

Ulises stepped into his apartment, pausing for a few seconds in the doorway to take in the particular atmosphere you encounter when you burst into a place knowing you're alone. The tar-like silence that's easy to find in homes where there are no children or pets.

He locked the door. He walked over to the box that was still in the middle of the hall and set down the bag he was carrying there, too.

Juan had come into Don Paco's room at six thirty in the morning to wake Ulises up, and had offered him a lift. Ulises opened his eyes, still a bit groggy. He had fallen asleep on the recliner that Don Paco had opposite his bed. A chair, he thought at the time, identical to the one in the Los Argonautas library.

And the bed was empty.

"What about Don Paco?" he asked.

"In Galipán. He has his first coffee at five thirty in the morning and goes out to watch them shipping off the flowers."

They got into one of those rural four-wheel-drive pickups. They didn't talk much as they made their way down the mountain. The swaying and winding road meant that Juan had to focus on the driving and Ulises needed to be careful not to bump his head against the windshield. When they reached Cota Mil, Juan told him that those evening tours around the hotel were just messing about.

"Good money, though. They're the kids of military folks or government bigshots. I don't reckon you're supposed to do it, but we all got to make a living, right?"

"Of course you do," said Ulises.

Every so often, Juan would glance at the bag Ulises had on his lap.

"Where do you live?" asked Juan.

"Oh, you don't need to drive me home. I can get a cab," said Ulises, knowing he didn't have enough cash for that.

"I'll take you," Juan insisted. "Don Paco's orders."

The only things missing from the box were Señora Altagracia's manuscripts of the translations, which Nadine had taken. Ulises looked in the fabric bag again. The little wooden box Don Paco had given him was there. He checked that everything else was in order and closed the bag again.

He went to his bedroom. Nadine had slept out again. When Jesús called to tell him Segovia had died, he'd said he had found her over at the house very early. Judging by her face and clothes, it looked like she'd been partying all night and gone straight to Los Argonautas for breakfast. And now he had totally forgotten to let her know he was going to be spending the night at the Hotel Humboldt with Segovia's brother. *Such a crazy story. I'll tell you all about it tomorrow*, he would have texted if she were really his woman. So what was she? She hadn't texted to ask where he was either. And not asking at certain times of the day where or how the other person is, that's a sign of dislike or indifference in a city as dangerous as Caracas.

He felt sorry not to have a brother at the very least, as Paco and Facundo had been to each other. No bond that predated the mask of adulthood. No embarrassing memory tying him to somebody. No mirror in which the original light that a newborn encounters persists, and which we only notice when someone else retrieves it for us, like a coin taken out of a pond.

He showered and put on his pajamas. In the medicine cabinet, he found one of those powerful sleeping pills Paulina took before a flight, and lay down to sleep.

He woke up just after six the following morning, with a hunger pang that felt like an uppercut to his stomach. There was nothing for breakfast. He thought about Señora Carmen's arepas, and his mouth watered.

He called Los Argonautas. It was Jesús himself who answered the phone.

"I was about to call to see where you were," said Jesús.

"Morning, Jesús. I stayed at the apartment. Could you come fetch me, please?"

"OK. Give me the address and I'll head right out," said Jesús.

Before hanging up, Ulises asked:

"Is Nadine there?"

Jesús lowered his voice slightly.

"Yes, she woke up here," he said.

"What do you mean woke up?"

"Well, just like the day before yesterday. We couldn't talk because of all the chaos with Señor Segovia's death, but yeah. She was here very early in the morning when it happened. Didn't you know?"

"No. I didn't know."

Jesús raised his voice again and said:

"OK, I'll leave right now."

He picked him up, and as they drove back to Los Argonautas, Ulises learned what had happened: that Nadine had shown up in the garden just before dawn and danced.

"Like a ballerina," explained Jesús.

"What else does she do?" asked Ulises.

Jesús's hands tightened on the wheel, and he said:

"Well, I also saw her do something that looked like she was writing. You know, as if it was daytime and she was just there reading and writing."

"But was she awake?"

"Her eyes were open, although she did have a strange look in them. It was kind of scary, to be honest. Now that you ask, I don't know if she was awake, actually. Does she suffer from it?"

"From sleepwalking?"

"Uh-huh."

"I don't know," said Ulises. And then he added: "Not as far as I know."

When they went into the kitchen, Señora Carmen had two arepas and a cup of coffee waiting for him.

Ulises ate slowly, savoring every bite. When he finished, he took his plate to the sink, looked out the window, saw Nadine and asked:

"What's she doing?"

Señora Carmen dropped the tea towel she was using to dry a plate and came over.

"Some exercises, that's what Dr. Mariela says."

Ulises finished his coffee and went out into the garden. The dogs came running, tails wagging, to greet him. They were so excited that he had to stop to play with them. Fredo lay on his back, and Ulises scratched his belly. Then Michael and Sonny also lay on their backs, demanding the same treatment. He spent a few minutes petting them at short and intense intervals to keep them from getting impatient. How long had it been since he'd spent time with the dogs like this? Hadn't he always wanted one?

He saw Nadine lying on the grass, her head stretched back, watching him with just one eye. The mix of rage and sadness he'd been carrying with him since the call with Jesús suddenly dissipated. Michael, Sonny, and Fredo had attached themselves to him like suction cups and had sucked out and expelled all the discontent from his body.

They are like Christ, thought Ulises, as he walked toward Nadine. They bear the pain of others, but without the need for crucifixions or suffering. They only need their tails, and running about like crazy, to summon electromagnetic waves of joy. Dogs are like Christ but crazy, thought Ulises. They're Christs crazy with joy.

He stopped when he was level with Nadine's head. Their inverted faces watched each other like the yin and yang symbol.

"What are you doing?" he asked.

"I'm stretching my back," said Nadine.

"I've been thinking about something, tell me what you reckon," he announced, though it had only just occurred to him. "What do you say we move to Los Argonautas? At least for a while, till they finish the work."

Nadine closed her eyes, crossed her arms over her chest, and smiled.

"I think it's a wonderful idea," she said.

Ulises had never seen her look so beautiful.

25

Paco had settled into the rocking chair next to his bed. He'd offered Ulises a recliner.

"This picture is from 1956. I arrived in May, my brother in December," he said, handing over a yellow photograph showing the two men standing next to a woman.

Paco had first stowed away on a ship to New York, from where he'd boarded another ship bound for La Guaira, a harbor where many of his countrymen headed to escape from poverty. He hid in the entrails of some cranes that occupied most of the vessel's hold. During the journey, he heard that the machines were to be used on an important construction project in Caracas, the country's capital. When they finally reached La Guaira, Paco remained hidden. He slipped into a space he found between the cabin and the counterweights of one of the cranes and didn't set foot on land until they reached Maripérez, an area at the foot of the Ávila. He disembarked there and immediately looked for the foreman who, like him, happened to be Galician, albeit from Pontevedra, and offered to do whatever work was needed. The foreman gave him a wheelbarrow and Paco began to work as a barrow pusher.

"That crane was my ship, and Maripérez my harbor," said Paco. "And I haven't moved from here since."

Paco's room, in that blue hallway next to the machine room, was made up of two bedrooms converted into a single space. The walls were also blue, though of a lighter shade. The one at the back had three portholes that in the mornings let in the green stain of the mountain, and the blue-white stain that is Caracas bleeding into the sky above, making the room look like a ship's cabin. As if, in this room in the basement of the Hotel Humboldt, Paco had found a way to remain a stowaway for the rest of his life.

Back in his natural habitat, like a little fish moved from a bag of water into a tank, Paco had regained his youth and mobility. Not only did he walk faster and more upright now, but his words flowed with a clarity that would have been unimaginable in the old man who just hours earlier had seemed so utterly lost at his brother's funeral.

And now there was this, which Paco had just disclosed: since 1965, he had never again left that circuit. He had spent more than sixty years moving between the Hotel Humboldt and the Galician Brotherhood on Maripérez Avenue. The only times Paco would leave his fish tank were when, every so many years, he needed to renew his Spanish passport or sign a certificate confirming that he was currently alive.

"And now, because of Facundito's death," he said, when Ulises asked about this.

"And what do you do when you get ill?"

"I've never been ill. But we're not here for me to talk about myself. Let me fetch the parcel I have for you," he said and stood up.

"What parcel?" asked Ulises.

The old man was checking the shelves of an old bookcase bursting with magazines. He paused in front of some black-spined folders, took out two or three and threw them on the floor. They were like photo albums but filled with newspaper clippings. A few pages came loose on the bedroom floor.

"Do you need help?" asked Ulises.

"No," said Paco, "I'm almost done."

He reached his arm into the bookcase through what seemed to be a false wall, struggled for a few seconds, and finally pulled out a small wooden box. He settled back into his rocking-chair and handed it to Ulises.

"Here it is. Take it."

It was a rectangular box with the word *Cohiba* on the lid.

"Havana cigars? That's what Segovia left me?" said Ulises. "I don't even smoke."

The old man laughed.

"Open it."

Ulises opened the box and found a small plastic bag. He pulled out the bag and extracted what looked like a leather strap about ten centimeters long and four wide. On one end it had a broken buckle of thick, rusty metal. The other end was a stub that still showed the direction of the knife that had cut it.

"So? What do you make of that?" asked Paco.

"I don't get it. Is it a belt?"

"I'll give you a clue. It's not a belt. It's a collar."

"I see."

"Uh-huh," said Paco, now starting to rock himself faster. "But not any old collar. Nevado's collar."

Ulises still had to think hard for a bit until at last he saw the light.

"Bolívar's dog?"

"Uh-huh," said Paco again, rocking vigorously and smiling.

Ulises looked at that long ceiba-tree smile as it moved a few centimeters closer and then further again, to the rhythm of the rocking chair. A rocking chair made out of the bones of Señor Paco himself. Ulises looked toward the portholes. We're on the open seas, he thought. This is the only way to make a ship that is a house on top of a mountain.

The rocking chair went on moving and creaking.

He's hypnotizing me, thought Ulises. I must say something. Say something and act normal, that way you can get back.

"So it was true, then?" he said at last.

The rocking chair stopped.

"Course it's true. Well, that also depends on what my brother told you. Facundito did talk a lot of crap. He liked secrets. Even when there weren't any, he'd make them up. All he ever had to do was tell a story badly. Sort of sideways."

"I know what you mean," said Ulises. "He didn't tell me much, to be honest."

Paco smiled.

"That's Facundito for you. Who knows. Maybe he was trying to protect you."

"Protect me? From what?"

"I don't know. Last time we spoke, he said things weren't great at the house."

"That's what he said?"

"Yes."

"And he didn't say what wasn't going well?"

"No. But I'm telling you, Facundito was full of shit. Maybe he was just fooling around."

"Why did he ask you to give me this, then?"

"He didn't, but I know him. I'm certain that he held you in high regard."

"Paco, don't tell me you really believe this is Nevado's collar."

"This *is* Nevado's collar. It's even got a bloodstain."

Ulises turned the collar over and on the back, next to the cut, he found a large dark stain.

"But this stain could be anything," said Ulises.

"It could be anything, but it isn't. It's blood. What I don't yet know is if it's Nevado's blood. After all, what you're holding could even be the only existing sample of the blood of El Libertador Simón Bolívar himself."

With this, Paco resumed his rocking, more gently now. He yawned and closed his eyes.

"What do you mean El Libertador's blood, Don Paco?"

Without opening his eyes, Paco replied:

"It's a long story. I'm going to rest for a little bit."

He went on gently rocking. He propelled the chair with the lightest brush of the flip-flops he wore on his feet, barely touching the floor. Feet, Ulises noticed, that were huge, with gnarled toes and long ivory toenails.

26

By the end of the week of Segovia's death, Ulises and Nadine had moved to Los Argonautas. They bought a mattress, a set of sheets, and a set of towels, and took over a room that could be reached from the third floor via a staircase. The room had a sort of hatch that led onto the roof of the house.

"This is our loft," Ulises told her.

They had privacy there, and no longer needed to travel through the city every morning. Señora Carmen prepared their coffee and meals. Ulises made better use of his time and was able to provide more help to Jesús and Mariela. And Nadine was in the garden, where she had established her kingdom.

Between Elizabeth von Arnim's books, which she loved, and Altagracia's translations, which were very painstaking, Nadine had been assembling a series of elements that set her on track for a real discovery: among the footnotes, which were a conversation with Elizabeth scattered with grammatical and lexical explications; among Altagracia's sometimes too-free rendering of certain passages; among all those traces that sketch out the ever elusive shadow of the translator, Nadine recognized the notes toward what perhaps could be Altagracia's memoirs.

As for Ulises, he was focused on speeding up the work that

was needed to get the foundation open on time. Which did seem possible, given the progress they were making. The temporary kennels had already been set up in two big rooms on the second floor, as had the basic furnishings of the clinic. They had commissioned and signed off on the Simpatía por el Perro logo. They had been in touch with a journalist who was already planning a press campaign around the foundation's launch and managing their social media. The graphic designer put them in touch with a web developer, who would have a presentable version of foundation's official site on time. Mariela was scheduling interviews with the vets who would start working with them. And despite their short time living at Los Argonautas, they had already made a difference in the team's performance. At least, that's what Ulises liked to think. The only detail they hadn't heard about yet, which worried Jesús especially, regarded the purchase of medical equipment, medicines, and dog food.

"Without that, we can't really launch," said Jesús. "There's less than six weeks left. Closer to five, actually."

"Let me call Aponte," said Ulises.

How had he forgotten? He blamed the house. He'd become distracted wandering around it. Just when he thought he knew all the nooks and crannies, a new room, hallway, or attic appeared. Sometimes a whole wing would be on the left side, instead of the right, as he thought he remembered. As if during the night, or even during the day, the house rearranged itself according to some unknown logic.

He had not, for example, found the hideout from which he'd seen Segovia emerging. He had felt around the library floor, as well as the ceiling of the security room, as Segovia had called the space between the kitchen and the storeroom from where the CCTV was controlled, and which was underneath the library. All to no avail. There was no way some hidden passage could exist between the two places, through which Segovia or anyone else could secretly pass. Had he dreamed it? But his box was still there, in the hall of his apartment, together with the cigar box which contained a fragment of a leather collar, which not only belonged to Nevado, El Libertador's dog, but was stained with the blessed blood of Simón Bolívar himself. And yet, he couldn't find the passage Segovia had used. Nor could he understand why he had given him, almost as his dying wish, the two boxes.

Life at Los Argonautas had become so pleasant that everything relating to the mystery of Segovia and his brother Paco had been rendered absurd. How could Segovia have insinuated, just because of Paulina's dirty trick of hiring a drunk psychiatrist, that there was some threat looming over the house? Perhaps the old man was merely foreshadowing his own death, Ulises thought.

He went to the kitchen and made himself some tea. It was three in the afternoon and Carmen was resting in her room. Ulises looked out the window as he waited for the drink to cool. He saw his girlfriend in the garden, advancing into the territory of a single book. He drank two sips of tea and dialed Aponte's number. As the phone rang, he went to the security room.

Aponte didn't answer. Ulises' recliner in the library was in the exact spot where he was standing, only upstairs. So Segovia's hideout ought to be in the next-door room, but there was nothing there but a pantry for storing food.

His phone rang.

"Aponte, how's everything?"

"Nonstop, as always. I was about to call you. What's up?"

"I wanted to know what's happened with the equipment."

"The equipment arrived at La Guaira two days ago. I've just been notified. But there's a problem at customs. We need to make a decision. And you've only got four weeks left."

"Five weeks, Aponte. We have just over five weeks."

"Well, whatever. I also wanted to talk to you about something else. Paulina has gotten back in touch."

"What for?"

"Let's get lunch, and I'll tell you then."

They arranged to meet up the following day. After hanging up, Ulises just kept looking at the ceiling. Had he seen that crack before? He heard the dogs barking, play-biting, and chasing each other, then Nadine's voice telling them to be quiet. And he remembered what he hadn't yet dared ask Nadine. The question that Michael, Sonny, and Fredo's loving assault had made him completely forget: How had she arrived at Los Argonautas so early in the morning?

Ulises began to work the controls, but only succeeded in turning off the cameras. He walked over to Señora Carmen's room and knocked on her door.

"Sorry to bother you, Carmen, but do you know where I can find the instructions for the security cameras?"

"Let me show you."

Señora Carmen's room was on the east wing of the first floor of the house. A wing that had been sort of abandoned, since the activity in Los Argonautas, even in the years before General Ayala's death, had focused around the center, where the kitchen was, and the west wing. Though it was hardly advisable to be apart from the rest of the house at her age, Señora Carmen preferred to stay where she had always lived.

Ulises was surprised when, on their walk back from her

room, the corridor took an unexpected turn and they came upon a door he had never seen before. Carmen took a bunch of keys from the front pocket of her uniform, opened the door, and went in.

"This was Señora Altagracia's studio. When she wasn't in the garden, she'd spend the day here reading, writing, and painting."

It was a small room. There was no furniture, only a row of folders lined up against one of the walls. The wall at the back was covered by some awful office blinds, and, high up, an old air-conditioning unit. Ulises stepped forward, pulled the cord, and rolled up the blinds, revealing a courtyard the size of a large balcony.

"It used to be full of flowers. Even prettier than the ones in the other garden."

The other garden, Ulises thought. The larger one, the visible one, had always been "the other," with respect to some original version, something smaller, hidden, and faithful.

Señora Carmen opened one of the folders and said:

"Come here."

Ulises took two steps and stood behind her.

"General Pinzón kept everything. General Ayala, too. Any papers you might need are here. Invoices, receipts, copies of documents, everything. Instructions and warranties for every gadget in the house are also here. See this folder, that says *Manuals & warranties for appliances, etc.*? What you're looking for must be here."

"Perfect."

According to the manual, the cameras were configured to store the recordings for fourteen days, after which the memory was automatically erased.

He went back to the kitchen and took another look at the garden. Nadine, her position practically unchanged, was still reading. Then he went to the security room and, following the instructions, began to handle the controls. He accessed the recording log and backtracked to the early morning of Segovia's death. He checked from midnight onward. The recording didn't show any activity whatsoever. It was the only house on a cul-de-sac in a development where most of the villas were vacant. Now and then, some stray cat would make him pause the footage. He forwarded the tape until some lights in the background disturbed the stillness of the image. The timestamp read 3:37 a.m. That was when a car approached, and stopped right across the street. Ulises could see Nadine getting out from the passenger seat, leaving the car door open, walking to the main gate, and going in. From inside the car, the driver pulled the passenger door closed. The car turned around and drove away.

The same scene was repeated on the night of Segovia's funeral, with just twelve minutes' difference. At 3:49 in the morning, the camera showed Nadine getting out of the same car: a black Toyota Corolla.

27

While Paco snored, Ulises started to look over the bookshelves. On one side, there were old magazines about science, occultism, and science fiction. On the other, the black folders full of newspaper clippings ordered thematically, with yellowish labels precariously attached to the spines and identified with a marker that had once been black. Ulises pulled out one that said *Ávila/Volcano*. The folder contained lots of articles and features about an old Caracas legend: that deep in the bowels of the Ávila, there was a hidden volcano that would one day transform Caracas into a new Pompeii.

He found the news story, clipped from the front page of *El Universal*, about the breakdown of the cable car at the Maripérez station on August 7, 1977. One of the main cables got stuck in one of the pulleys and began to fray. Cabins filled with passengers were left hanging for several hours over the green abyss. Many had to be taken off via the section of the cable car that leads to Macuto, down the other side of the mountain and overlooking the sea. After that day, the cable car was "closed until further notice" and the hotel entered one of its longest periods of disuse.

On the next page, there was a feature from *El Nacional*, published on Monday, August 22, 1977, under the headline "The Day Ávila Was Going to Split in Two . . . But Didn't," and with the byline L. Medina. It was a gripping account of how the city emptied out that weekend when faced with the threat of the Ávila cracking into two halves and opening the way to the waters of the Caribbean Sea, prompting a colossal flood. The horrific vision was spread by a man who swore he had met a prophet in dark glasses on the street foretelling the cataclysm.

From the juxtaposing of the two clippings, one would have thought Don Paco might have made a connection between the closing of the cable car and the belief that a volcano hidden in the Ávila was finally going to erupt. But the only note Don Paco had made at the bottom of the story of August 22, 1977, was a sort of bibliographic record and some page numbers. On the wall at the back of the bookshelves, Ulises found labels with a handwritten alphanumeric code. This was a filing system Paco had improvised for his personal newspaper archive. Ulises located the magazine that the card referred to. It was also an August issue, but from 1969, of a bilingual German-Venezuelan publication called *Venessuela*. The cover was predominantly red and black, and instead of the letter *z* there was a pair of *s*'s in the shape of swastikas.

Was Don Paco a Nazi? Could that explain his isolation? It wouldn't make much sense, since he was a Republican and had fled Franco's Spain. Or so he said.

Ulises searched for the specified pages in the magazine. The article was entitled "Ein U-Boot im Guaire-Fluss / A Submarine on the Guaire River," and it gave an account of the expedition of a German submarine, the *Gnade*, off the Venezuelan coast during World War II. Apparently, its mission was to probe the waters of what had been the only German colony in America, with a view to regaining it. Because that's what the article noted: that between 1528 and 1545, Charles I of Spain had granted the bankers of Augsburg's Welser family the Klein-Venedig province—or Little Venice, as Venezuela had been known since the time of Amerigo Vespucci—as payment for the debt he had incurred on his quest to become Charles V, Holy Roman Emperor.

One thing we know for sure: the submarine vanished. It's been said that this was the only German submarine to get torpedoed on February 16, 1942, when the Kriegsmarine's U-502 sank the oil tanker *Monagas* just off the Paraguaná Peninsula. This has never been verified. The author of this article, who didn't use a byline, gave an account of the events that, while he didn't believe them to be true, still seemed to give him an alarming amount of pleasure. The *Gnade* might have come too close to the Macuto coast and been swallowed up by a very strong undercurrent which, after some indeterminate time, hurled it onto the riverbed of the Guaire. How had the *Gnade* managed to pass directly beneath the mountain? Well, through one of the several underwater channels hidden in the Ávila, as might be inferred from certain notes made by the Jesuit Athanasius Kircher in his famous 1665 work *Mundus subterraneus*. A massive hole that, *like Scylla and Charybdis dragging down Ulysses and his companions, ended up pulling the submarine until it was thrown straight into the city's river artery*. What happened to the *Gnade* afterwards? It never reappeared, although some witnesses from '45 swore that on their nighttime wanderings along the banks of the Guaire, they'd seen a whale's body suddenly surfacing from the river's depths.

From this forum of critical thought against the shameful world order that rules us, the article concluded, *we do not rule out the possibility that this was the* Gnade, *an iron cetacean and a symbol of the coming rebirth of the great German nation, not on the lifeless ground of a Europe that has betrayed its origins, but in Venezuela: the first German bastion in the New World.*

After checking other sections in the bookshelves, it was clear that, even if Don Paco was a Germanophile, this did not make him into a follower of Hitler. Next to issues of *Venessuela* magazine, there were also cultural publications with excerpts of *Travels to the Equinoctial Regions* by Baron Alexander von Humboldt, or *Tales from the Secret Annex* by Anne Frank. In that book, Don Paco had highlighted a quote from September 29, 1942: *The strangest things happen to you when you're in hiding.* Apart from highlighting it with a pen, Paco had also copied it onto a square of paper that he had glued onto the same page of the supplement.

Did Don Paco identify himself with the Jews, then? Or just with Anne Frank, for the mere fact of having been "in hiding" like her?

Ulises went on rummaging through the library and found a folder marked *Hotels.* He took it out and sat back in his reclining chair. It was a collection of articles about the most famous hotels in Caracas. Hotel Humboldt featured at the end of the first section, but its entry was just an asterisk with the note: *To read about the Hotel Humboldt, go to the special volume AV/HUMB/19/Sec.ÁVILA.*

This wasn't just a newspaper archive. It was a kind of hand-crafted Google that Paco had assembled over decades, turning the small world of his obsessions into an inexhaustible universe, its links made out of cards and handwritten notes, carrying you from one place to the next, from one reference to the next, always within the limits of Caracas. This spiderweb of news, features, and interconnected articles was a scale reproduction of the city, and of Don Paco's own life.

Ulises replaced the folder and went on looking at others. He found one that was unidentified. It did not contain newspaper articles. It was the manuscript of a science fiction novel written by Francisco Segovia entitled *The Year of Mercy*. And in parentheses: *An apocalyptic science fiction novel that can be used as a spell to prevent the events narrated here from happening in a not-too-distant future.*

He heard the rocking chair shifting from its barely audible sound of hibernation, caused by the slightest rocking that Don Paco sustained like a heartbeat while he slept, to a louder creaking sound. He put the folder down on the shelf and returned to the recliner. After a cough that exploded like the exhaust of a rickety old car, Paco woke up mumbling gibberish that became gradually clearer as he came around. It was like an old radio being tuned in by some higher power. And so, as if the pause had lasted no longer than the blink of an eye, Paco resumed the conversation at the point where they had left off. But before explaining the thing about the Libertador's bloodstain on Nevado's collar, he needed to tell Ulises how he had first met General Martín Ayala.

"Because if I start out by telling you what comes later, you won't understand a thing."

28

Aponte arranged to meet him at La Parada, a restaurant in Los Palos Grandes near the Cuadra Gastronómica mall.

"It's the Boliboys who come to this place, rather than the Chavistas. They've got a different lineage. Boliboys are the grandchildren of the guys who stole when Pérez Jiménez was in power, who in turn are the grandchildren of those who stole when Gómez was."

"Oh, and nobody stole when the 'adecos' were in power, right?"

"Sure they did, but what the Chavistas and Boliboys have stolen, that's a whole other level. These guys are the great leaders in swindling. They're the Bolívar, Páez, and Urdaneta of corruption. Stealing on this scale has only happened a few times in history, and not just this country's history, but anywhere. That's why they'd rather see Venezuela left without two stones piled on top of one another than release their prey."

Ulises nodded and took his cellphone out of his pocket. Absentmindedly, he set it down on the table.

"Would you like me to recommend something from the menu?" asked Aponte.

"Order for both of us. And I'll just drink water. I'm swamped with the jobs in the house, and I'm going there right after this to try to sort a lot of stuff out. I really want to meet the deadline. And I think we will make it. The problem, like I said, is the equipment. Without the equipment and the sacks of dog food, we're fucked."

"I understand, but let's order first," Aponte said, and he called over a waiter. "I'm ordering salmon—it's always fresh here—so that we'll be eating something light."

Aponte stretched out the conversation until they brought in the dishes. Then he started talking, between bites.

"Paulina called me, like I said. She wants me to help her recover the house and the apartment."

"Recover them? They never belonged to her!"

"I'm just telling you what she said."

"OK. And what did you say?"

"I told her I wasn't the executor of the will."

"Didn't she know that already?"

"Yes, and I repeated it. And she insisted. You'll understand me if I tell you she made me an offer I can hardly refuse."

Aponte stopped talking and carried on eating, his eyes fixed on his plate.

"What offer?" asked Ulises.

"She offered me the apartment in exchange for helping her get the house."

This time, Aponte looked him in the eye. Ulises couldn't help glancing at the entrance and then at his cellphone.

"She's not in Caracas. Don't worry. What do you think this is, an ambush?"

"And what am I supposed to say? It's still your father who's going to execute the will. Has he changed his opinion, by any chance?"

"Oh, not at all. However, I fear his health hasn't been that good lately. It'd be a shame if the old man were to die all of a sudden, leaving us all up in the air."

"Last time we met, you said your father was fit as an ox."

"He is, but you always have those imponderables of life. Especially when you're over eighty-one. One day you feel fine, the next you don't. I mentioned this to Paulina and guess what, she gave me power of attorney to execute her father's will in the event of my old man kicking the bucket."

"They're not insisting on the annulment anymore?"

"Doesn't seem like it."

"Well, I can see you're clear about everything. So why did you ask to meet?"

"Because it's important that you know. I've always been transparent with you. I don't like surprises. Also, I needed to tell you that I might not listen to Paulina. I'm sure you'll make me a better offer."

Ulises pushed the plate aside.

"What the fuck are you talking about?"

"Ulises, I'm not interested in the apartment. I want the house. You could do a lot with a piece of land like that. What about a hotel there?"

Ulises thought about Don Paco's folders and the Hotel Humboldt.

"A hotel in the desert. Oh, why not?" he said.

"In the desert? A hotel right next to Los Chorros Park! In the foothill of the Ávila. Just imagine! There might be something for you, too."

"I don't follow."

"If it were to happen, God forbid, that my old man died and I became the executor of the will, I would keep the house and you, the apartment."

"But the apartment is mine."

"It's not yours. It's *almost* yours. Only now you risk being left with nothing. Which is why—and to show you that I'm conscious of your situation—I'm offering you, in addition to the apartment, a small bonus when I get possession of the house. You just need to sign a letter of agreement indicating the handover of the house to a foundation in my name, since you're going to appear as one of the directors in the articles of incorporation for the Simpatía por el Perro Foundation. And this certificate will take effect the day the foundation opens, once it's been verified that everything has been completed as agreed."

"And what if it turns out your old man is in better shape than you think, and in the end, I manage to open the foundation?"

"In order to get the foundation open on time, the equipment and the entire order of medicines and food would have to be released at customs. One phone call from me, you'll have them in the house next week. The problem is, I might lose the contact I have in La Guaira. Just like that, all of a sudden."

"The imponderables of life."

"Exactly, Ulisito. You got it."

"Don't call me that."

Aponte raised his hands as if in surrender and burst out laughing.

"I get why you're upset. The foundation is very nice, and it's philanthropic, but do you actually know how many dogs are abandoned every day? Hundreds! And that's just in Caracas. Imagine in the rest of the country. Must be thousands. What difference does it make if you rescue just a few? Besides, if you end up losing the apartment, what would the point of all these years have been?"

"What do you mean?"

"You never fooled Martín, Ulises. That was only later, when he became even madder and ended up adopting you like a puppy, just to screw over his children. In fact, you were the last puppy rescued in that house. But the truth was, Martín knew you married Paulina for the apartment."

Ulises turned pale.

"So, what do you say?" asked Aponte.

"How long have I got?"

"If I don't hear from you by two weeks before the opening, I'll have no choice but to talk to Paulina. Get it?"

"Got it," said Ulises.

"Great. Now, do me a favor and give me your PIN so we can delete all the shit you've been recording."

Swiftly, Aponte grabbed Ulises' phone and he was now holding it up to show him the locked screen with the recorder app running.

Ulises stammered a number. Aponte entered the code, stopped the recording, and deleted the file. As he continued to look through the phone, he said:

"They're already advertising the latest iPhone. Apparently, the camera is great, and so's the recorder. It can record even when it's inside a bag. Next time."

Aponte handed the phone over, wiped his mouth on the cloth napkin, and gestured to Ulises that he could leave.

Ulises was trembling when he arrived at the parking lot. He got into his car and started the engine. He took out the cellphone and threw it onto the passenger seat. Still shaken, he patted the inside pocket of his jacket and pulled out his old Android with its cracked screen and broken case. He unlocked it, opened the recorder, and pressed Stop. He labelled the file *Aponte*, and clicked Save. Then he turned the volume all the way up, pressed Play and drove off. Despite not having used the latest iPhone, his conversation with Dr. Edgardo Aponte had recorded very well.

29

The Caracas cable car and the Hotel Humboldt facilities had changed hands many times. After its opening in 1956, the hotel remained active until 1961. From then on, and over the following decades, it would be closed, or reopened, during periods coinciding with the country's peaks and troughs of hope and despair. The Humboldt was the Venezuelan people's *Titanic*. Only it was a very particular ship. It was a ship born already grounded atop the mountain, a ship that would never sink completely, and which would never set sail.

In March 1998, when Chávez began to lead in the presidential polls, the Venezuelan State decided to privatize the cable car and the hotel. A consortium took control of both, and proceeded to modernize them. They refurbished the cable system, the generators, the cabins, and the cable car stations, as well as remodeling and redesigning the recreational areas. The tourist development was christened Ávila Mágica, and carried on until 2007, when the government expropriated it.

Paco Segovia had survived all the changes of management. One of the most difficult had happened in 1977, when the Venezuelan Tourism Corporation was created. Paco was allowed to stay on in the hotel, but without an agreed salary. He lived on his savings for a few months, until he was granted a pension from Spain. The pension was more than enough to cover his expenses, which were limited to the odd lunch at the Galician Brotherhood and his magazine subscriptions.

The second most difficult moment happened thirty years later, with the expropriation of Ávila Mágica. A secretary at the Ministry of Tourism informed him not only that he wasn't going to be paid a salary, something Paco hadn't asked for, but that he would also have to vacate the room he had been living in for so many years.

Paco dialed the telephone number of General Pinzón's house in distress. He knew that General Pinzón was dead, but dialing that number was the only thing he could think of at that moment. Paco's call came on a melancholy afternoon just as Martín Ayala was wandering the deserted house, pondering the pros and cons of shooting his wife and then blowing his own brains out. His last argument with Altagracia had caused her to lock herself in her studio, and she hadn't come out for three weeks. Carmen took her food, but there was one occasion when Altagracia went without eating for over a day because she suspected he was behind the door, trying to see her; as indeed he had been. Martín was so worried that he shouted through the door that he wouldn't do it again. And it was only then that Altagracia agreed to let Carmen in and to go back to eating, but the days went by, and still she didn't come out, while Martín went mad with sorrow and loneliness.

So when he heard that old and sullen voice on the phone introducing itself as the "keeper of the Humboldt," Martín could not help but pay attention.

"Keeper of the Humboldt? How so?"

"Well, señor, I look after the Hotel Humboldt. The hotel that's here on the Ávila—you know the one?"

"Alright. And how can I help you?"

"Well, señor, the government has just taken possession of the hotel, and they want to throw me out. Me, who's been taking care of it since it opened."

"You've been there since Pérez Jiménez?"

"Yes, señor."

Things were getting fun.

"Well, señor, I'm very sorry they'd do that to you, of all people. Can you tell me your name?"

"Francisco Segovia, at your service. But you can call me Paco."

"As I was saying, I'm very sorry you're going through this, Señor Paco, but I'm not sure what all this has to do with me. So long."

"Just a moment, señor, please. I know that General Pinzón is dead now, but I don't know what else to do."

When he heard General Pinzón's name, Martín held on to the receiver and carried on listening. Finally he understood what was happening. The next morning, Martín went to the cable car.

There was an employee waiting at Maripérez station to accompany him in the cabin during his ascent. And when they arrived at the Ávila station, the man led him to the door of Paco Segovia's room.

That day, Martín and Paco had lunch together. Before leaving, Martín promised he'd have an answer soon.

Two days later, Paco received a call from the same secretary at the Ministry of Tourism, notifying him that he could stay in his room at the Humboldt.

"Moreover, on the instructions of the Commander-in-Chief, Hugo Chávez, you will be granted a pension by the Venezuelan government in recognition of your many years of service."

At the end of that same week, an alarmed Señora Carmen woke Martín from his nap, to inform him that there was a man with a dog at the front gate.

"With a dog? Tell him to go away."

"I did tell him, but he insists it's a gift for you. The dog is huge."

Martín tidied himself up a bit and went out to the gate to see what was going on. There he saw the same man who had met him at the cable car. He was holding a chain attached to a collar around the neck of a dog that was indeed huge. His fur was all black but for a line of white hair that ran down his spine like snow on the mountain ranges.

"General, this is Nevadito. It's a gift from Don Paco to thank you for the favor you did him."

The man held out the chain. Martín took it, mumbling that it must have been a mistake.

"You'll find Nevadito's papers in this folder, vaccines and all. Have a good day, general."

He got into a jeep which still had the Ávila Mágica logo visible on one of its doors and drove off without waiting for an answer.

Martín went inside, and the first thing the dog did was to take a long piss in the living room.

Señora Carmen came out of the kitchen and gave a yell when she saw what the animal was doing.

"What are you going to do with that dog, general?"

Martín stared at the puddle of urine that Nevadito had left on the parquet, and watched the liquid make its sinuous way under the kitchen's swinging door.

"You'll see what I'm going to do, Carmen. Come with me."

Martín placed his hand on the animal's enormous head and

encouraged him to follow. The three of them walked through
the house toward the east wing. After a while, they stopped
at the door of Altagracia's studio. Martín gestured to Señora
Carmen to knock.

"What is it?" Altagracia's voice sounded irritated as she
always was when interrupted.

They heard her footsteps drawing near. Altagracia opened
the door and stifled a scream when she saw the dog.

"What's this?" she said, her eyes alight with a mix of anger
and helplessness.

The dog, hearing Altagracia's voice, got up and began to wag
his tail. Martín held out the chain and said:

"His name's Nevadito."

30

Nadine had come to the conclusion that the traces that Altagracia left behind in her translations were deliberate. Those interstitial additions, apparent misreadings, and poetic licenses were the crumbs that led to her own life's secret story.

In one of her recurring comparisons between dogs and men, in which the latter always lost out, Elizabeth said the following:

> *I needed a companion. My husband still went off directly after breakfast to his distant farms, and the mornings, when I had done weighing-out sausages and counting sheets—for by now my responsibilities had been faced and accepted—were long. I needed something that had to be exercised, and therefore gave me an excuse for getting off to the woods myself; and since I still was young—it took me a terrible time to leave off being young— the companion couldn't be a pleasant youth, as I might perhaps have liked, because that would have set the Frau Director and the Frau Inspector and the Frau Vieharzt too much agog, but must be something beyond the reach of calumny.*

"Does Frau mean Señor?" asked Ulises.

"Señora. She's referring to the governess, the housekeeper, and the village vet. But don't interrupt me. Listen."

Nothing is so entirely beyond the reach of calumny as dogs; in fact, they seem to have all the privileges and exemptions that are most worth having. Ingraban and I could spend whole days together, and at night he could sleep on the rug by my bed, without a word being said. He was a Great Dane; a huge, lovely beast, of the colour called isabelle. I got him from a breeder in the nearest big town, and he was one of a series, born of the same parent, whose names all began with I.

"That's beautiful," Ulises said.

"Gorgeous. But now look at Altagracia's footnote in her translation: *Poor N. and I didn't even have that privilege.* Isn't that totally weird? I get the sense Altagracia had a lover," said Nadine.

"A relationship with a dog?"

"Don't be so literal."

Ulises was about to tell her that Altagracia did have a dog, and that the *N* must stand for Nevadito, but he remembered the early morning black Toyota Corolla and decided to keep quiet.

That footnote set Nadine off on an investigation about which she didn't reveal a thing. She asked him to order her a biography of Elizabeth von Arnim on Amazon. It was a book published in 1986, now out of print, the only available copies of which cost $200. She was so insistent that Ulises ended up emailing Aponte and asking him to buy the book, claiming it was essential for them to create content for the website. *I need it right away. I hope there are no problems at customs,* Ulises wrote at the end of his email. To which Aponte replied two hours later: *Hahaha. Don't worry. Just bought it. It should arrive next week. Keep in touch.*

When she heard, Nadine brightened up and gave him a kiss. Ulises pulled her down onto on the mattress in the loft.

"I'm not in the mood," she stopped him.

"Do you want me to go down on you?"

"I don't want that either. I need to get this done."

"Then tell me what it's about, at least."

"Not yet."

Some nights later, Ulises dreamed that Nadine was inserting a gold coin into her vagina. He began to lick it, and Nadine's vagina turned into a cave. Inside, Ulises stumbled upon a row of stones. The biggest was a tombstone with the letter *N* on it. Then the blue eyes of a cat tore through the darkness. Ulises followed the cat until he came to a ladder. He took his phone out of his pocket and activated the flashlight. He saw the box on the upper steps. He pointed the light toward the ceiling and saw a closed hatch. He picked up the box and climbed the remaining steps of the ladder to reach the hatch. Now he was in the library. He had found Segovia's hideout at last. Sitting on the recliner, with its black fur and blue eyes, was the cat.

When Elizabeth von Arnim's biography finally arrived, Nadine resumed her research with a vengeance. This time around, she wasn't even in the garden, but upstairs in the loft, which she wouldn't leave till the late afternoon when the dogs' insistent barking drew her out.

In the last of Altagracia's three manuscripts, Nadine found a title she hadn't previously noticed: *The Murder of the Man of Wrath*. She checked the index of her translation and couldn't find it. She went back to the third book, leafed back and forth through the pages, and located it. *The Murder of the Man of Wrath* came after the novel *Introduction to Sally* and before *Expiation*. At first, she thought it was an oversight on Altagracia's part. She looked for the white book, checked the index of novels and couldn't find it there either. She checked index against index. Altagracia had followed the sequence of the novels, which in the English version had been ordered according to the chronology of their first editions. The novel *The Murder of the Man of Wrath* didn't appear in the original. Moreover, its almost one hundred pages were the only ones in the three thick manuscripts that weren't numbered.

Nadine began to read the novel, which opened like a secret passageway between Elizabeth's novels and Altagracia's translations. The novel, the genre of which was specified in parentheses after the title, had an epigraph by Elizabeth von Arnim, reinforcing the hypothesis that the text actually belonged to Altagracia. The phrase was taken from her memoirs, and it was a mission statement: *A widow is the only complete example of her sex. In fact, the finished article.*

"It's an amazing novel. It's like reading von Arnim, except it's set in Caracas rather than Pomerania. And instead of her German garden, it's our garden."

"And Altagracia is Elizabeth, and Martín's the Man of Wrath," Ulises said.

"Yes."

"I see. And I guess it's my turn to be the Man of Wrath now."

Suddenly, Nadine burst out crying.

"Hey, what's wrong?"

"Nothing," she said when she calmed down. "Nothing at all."

At that moment, the dogs began to bark, and Nadine went

down out of the loft. The Caracas sky was revealing the usual purple clemency of its sunsets.

María Elena, Ulises thought.

If only he had dared to say those two words.

31

When he woke up, Nadine had already left the room. Elizabeth von Arnim's white book, as well as Altagracia's three translation manuscripts and the notebooks were still lying on the floor by her side of the bed. Ulises went down to the kitchen, took the coffee that Señora Carmen offered him, and having had his first sip, looked out the window.

"Have you seen Nadine?" he asked.

Señora Carmen, Jesús, and Mariela were focusing on their steaming cups, and they shook their heads in silence.

He could check the security cameras and find out when and how Nadine had left the house. Whether it was in the black Corolla, on foot or even in a different car. He did not. He didn't need an accurate picture. Ulises thought about his notebook, which he had left in the apartment. How long had he been going on like this, working every day, nonstop? Time at Los Argonautas seemed a succession of misshaped rooms, like the house itself.

"I'm going to the apartment to check that everything's OK there. Call if you need me," he said.

Now they all snapped out of the spell of the coffee.

"Don't worry," said Mariela.

"Go and rest," advised Jesús.

"I'll put your lunch in a little container for you, Señor Ulises," said Señora Carmen.

Maybe that's what a home was, he thought. Wanting to leave a place, just so you can come back.

He composed the following scene in his notebook:

Nadine's absence was final. It had been read in the grounds of the morning coffee. Señora Carmen was the first to notice it.

"It's the profile of the girl Nadia," she said, looking at the bottom of the cup. Señora Carmen had never been able to call her Nadine.

Ulises finished his coffee and there, in the bottom of his cup, he saw Nadine's profile. Ulises and Carmen compared cups and were stunned to see the same silhouette.

"Oh my God!" said Mariela. "It's in mine, too."

And she showed them the cup. Jesús was the only one who hadn't drunk his coffee yet. He had no choice but to finish it.

The fourth profile, or the fourth replica of the profile, was also there.

It could mean only one thing: death. But nobody uttered the word. Not even Carmen, the housekeeper, who knew how to read coffee grounds.

Nadine didn't come back that night, and nobody at Los Argonautas could get to sleep. Ulises got up at four in the morning. He took a chair from the kitchen, went to the security room, and sat down to wait. The black Corolla with the tinted windows appeared at 4:40, parking across the street. Ulises' heart was beating fast. He was sure he'd see Nadine getting out of the car, leaving the passenger door open, walking toward the main gate, and coming into the house.

However, some minutes went by, and Nadine did not get out. He heard some noise from the staircase.

"Who's that?" he asked.

"It's me," said Jesús. "Where are you?" Though what Jesús really wanted to ask was, What are you doing there? since he had already seen that he was in the security room. Behind him stood Mariela. The three of them began to watch the screen together.

"It's the same black car from last time," said Mariela.

They heard the dragging of sandals and saw Señora Carmen, with huge bags under her eyes, walking over to them without a word of greeting.

Several minutes went by without any activity outside.

"I'm going to make some coffee," said Señora Carmen. That was her solution to everything. Or when she didn't know what else to do.

"I'm going outside to find out what's going on," said Ulises.

They tried to discourage him, but in vain. Jesús made to follow, but Mariela begged her husband to stay inside.

Señora Carmen decided to watch what was happening on the screen in the security room. From there, she saw Señor Ulises opening the main gate, looking both ways, crossing the sidewalk, and knocking on the driver's window. Ulises had put his hands back into the pockets of his overalls. The two men exchanged some words. Ulises gestured toward the house. The man in the car turned off the inside light, rolled up his window and got out. The two men came inside.

Señora Carmen went back to the kitchen and put the kettle on.

"This gentleman is Nadine's husband," Ulises announced.

They tried to disguise the awkwardness of the situation and introduced themselves. The gentleman said a name that after-

wards, when they were discussing and reconstructing the scene, no one could remember.

"Let's go to the library," Ulises said. "Carmen, bring us some coffee, please."

Ulises and Nadine's husband, or María Elena's, since that's how the man referred to her, talked until seven in the morning. They said very important things to each other. The man, at one point, broke down and started crying. In the end, they said goodbye with a hug. Ulises thought him a sweet man, but broken inside. He was tied to Nadine, or María Elena, for reasons that couldn't be explained. Sometimes one just decides that life is all about suffering for another person. Just like that. And only death, their own or the other person's, can break that tie.

María Elena, or Nadine, suffered from disturbances and disorders, of which sleepwalking was just one manifestation. These disorders would sometimes make her forget she had a husband and a daughter. The husband blamed it on her mother, who was really her grandmother. She was a monster, in his view. And he also blamed Sri Sri Ravi Shankar.

"Who?" asked Ulises.

"Sri Sri Ravi Shankar," repeated the husband. "A guru from India who María Elena met in an ashram."

According to the husband, Sri Sri Ravi Shankar brainwashed Nadine or María Elena and slept with her.

"And she never was the same afterwards," he said, sadly. "I don't know when she's asleep or awake anymore. I'm sure this man is controlling her remotely."

He's mad, Ulises thought. I can't trust a word he says. Though he is right about Nadine. She does embody that uncertainty he describes.

Once the man had left, Ulises, exhausted, threw himself

into the reclining chair. Señora Carmen, Jesús, and Mariela appeared at the door of the library.

"I'll tell you about it later."

Señora Carmen went over to the chair where Nadine's husband had been sitting. She picked up the cup of coffee that the man had left on the seat.

"What do you see?" Ulises asked Señora Carmen, who was probing the bottom of the cup with an entomologist's eye.

"Nothing. He didn't drink it."

Ulises checked the bottom of his own cup. He saw a strange shape. Something that looked like a volcano, or a dog's head.

32

After several hours' writing in his notebook, Ulises went for an early evening walk around the Santa Fe mall. He ate two slices of pizza at a market stall, looked around the deserted stores with windows either empty or displaying the same product repeated ad nauseam, and returned to his apartment.

He looked back over what he had written. That short text could arguably be considered his first short story. He still had to work on the opening. Somehow he needed to summarize the whole context around the story. The first scene in the kitchen was quite good, he thought. As was the conversation in the early hours of the morning with the man who loves a woman who doesn't love him back and is mad. But what he liked most was the ending. That cup of coffee left untouched, and therefore untranslatable, throwing the story's whole magical element into disarray. And the other cup, that of the Ulises character, with its canine or volcanic silhouette reminding us that the world is a postapocalyptic antenna that goes on transmitting signals even if no one receives them. Or that human beings are postapocalyptic animals who keep on trying to receive signals even if nothing, or nobody, is transmitting them anymore.

Signals, thought Ulises. Good title.

Leaving the cup full or emptying it. Taking life as it comes or sucking it dry. Proof of the existence of God could be found in either option, but so could the proof of His nonexistence. In this respect, Ulises' short story reached a perfect equilibrium. It was neither a sordid demonstration of the meaninglessness of life, nor the revelation of a secret harmony bringing opposite poles together. He had lived his life between those extremes, a life full of movies and books that weighed down the two pans of the scale in turn. When he felt overtaken by apathy, Ulises would devour documentaries about the Nazi Holocaust, about the Stalinist purges, or about the most horrific crimes in towns of the American Midwest that had gone unpunished. When he felt more optimistic, he would rewatch his favorite movies, *Forrest Gump*, *The Godfather*, or *Lion*, and he would reinforce his belief that every action and thought carries some weight in the world, and that there is somebody keeping track of what's been claimed, and what's been paid out.

Though sometimes he did drop his guard and return to books by Kafka, and then he'd get depressed. Kafka's resolution of the conflict was totally ruthless. God existed. That was not to be questioned. The real problem was the nature of God's character. In this sense, Kafka's novels, diaries, and letters were irrefutable. When He was in a good mood, God would turn you into a bug and lock you in a jar that was pretending to be a room, then forget about you forever. When He was in a bad mood, He'd pronounce you guilty, torture you with the waiting, giving you hope for a few days, and then sacrifice you. Like a dog.

Ulises thought about the coffee grounds in his story.

Kafka, Kan, K., vol-kano, he thought. Nadine, Martín, jardín.

He lay down on the hammock and had an uneasy sleep. He woke up half an hour later and went to his room. He undressed and lay down in bed. Before falling asleep, he texted Jesús: *I'll stay here tonight. See you tomorrow.*

He was so tired he didn't wait for a reply.

He slept until eight in the morning. When he woke up, there was a message from Jesús. *OK. Goodnight.* If Nadine had come back, Jesús would have said something.

Then a call came in. Ulises looked at the screen on his phone: *Señora Kando.*

She's dead, he thought.

"Good morning, Ulises. It's Señora Kando. I'm sorry to be calling so early."

"What's happened?"

"It's about María Elena."

She's dead, he repeated to himself.

"Tell me."

The voice on the other end of the line went quiet for a moment.

"I knew it would end badly," said Señora Kando at last, "but not like this. I was afraid I'd be killed. Or even you. Not the child. But he finally did it. He killed María Elena *and* the girl. And then he killed himself."

33

Leaving the house for the wake was a nightmare. Señora Carmen had begun to cry, saying she didn't want to go. Ulises hugged her and insisted it was important they went together.

"If we don't go together, then everything we've managed to do, it all goes to shit. Please, Señora Carmen."

Señora Carmen wiped her tears and agreed to go.

Then it was Mariela's turn.

"This house is cursed," she said suddenly, and collapsed into a fit of crying.

When they were finally in the car, Ulises couldn't get it to start.

"I can't do it," he said, his hands helpless on the steering wheel.

"I'll drive," said Jesús, getting out. He opened his door and, as if dealing with an old man, helped Ulises out and into the seat he had just vacated in the back.

They arrived at the chapel half an hour before it closed.

"I just hope the wreath gets here on time," said Ulises, checking his phone.

"I ordered it from the actual cemetery," said Jesús. "They guaranteed it would come first thing."

They walked up the entrance ramp, supporting each other, like a battalion, until they identified the chapel and broke ranks. Ulises remained in the front line of that hesitant troop and was the first to look inside. He took a few steps back.

"The three coffins are there," he said. His hands were shaking.

Mariela and Señora Carmen started to cry quietly. Jesús had turned pale and started to sweat.

"At least they're closed," added Ulises.

He turned around and went into the chapel. There were only six people inside. Behind the urns, there was the wreath sent by the foundation. It was the only one.

In loving memory of "Nadine", from her friends at Los Argonautas (Simpatía por el Perro Foundation), read the ribbon, written in those loathsome gaudy colors they always use on wreaths.

A much older woman identical to Nadine came over.

"You're Ulises," she said.

"Señora Kando?"

"You look just as I imagined."

Ulises didn't know what to say and got tearful. The woman hugged him and, in a matter of seconds, his suffering grew to the point where he lost all notion of what pain even was anymore. There was something healing about that hug, like the clean cut of a blade amputating an arm.

"Thank you for the wreath."

"Don't mention it. It's really nothing. And the words don't even come close to capturing how much we loved Nadine. What happened is horrible."

"They do capture it. Though I would have left Nadine just as it was, without the quotation marks."

The other five people took this moment to leave.

Now it's the three of them, and us, just two, thought Ulises, looking at the coffins.

"That's Roger's family," explained Señora Kando. "They were saying this is what wakes are like nowadays. So many people have gone. And it's getting harder and harder to get to the cemetery. And, well, with the lack of security, they also close earlier."

Ulises thought about Martín's wake, and especially about Segovia's funeral, just a few weeks ago. The attendees were people in small groups that broke into even smaller ones as they returned home.

"María Elena's mamá hasn't come either. She said the ticket from Paris to Caracas cost a fortune."

"Well, Señora Kando, you were her mother after all."

"I'm not saying it because of me. Or even because of María Elena. I'm saying it because of my own daughter, who's never going to forgive herself. It's a lie that someone else can just replace a person's father or mother. Let alone their children. Maybe God, but you'll never stop longing for the flesh. It's like an emptiness in the stomach, but here," said the lady, tapping the middle of her chest.

She was the one who cried this time. Ulises guessed it was his turn to hug her now, but he didn't.

"Let me introduce you to the people who work with me. They loved Nadine a lot, too," he said.

He stepped out of the chapel for a moment, looked into the central hall, and beckoned them in.

They were a trembling bunch as they approached. Carmen and Mariela hugged Señora Kando. Jesús was stiff. Within moments, they were all hugging and crying. No witness could have said they weren't a family. Ulises did the math and he could breathe again: they were five, and the others just three.

That evening, at Los Argonautas, Ulises spoke:

"No one is jumping ship. We are on track, and we will make it. We need to keep working just as we have been. And we'll carry on as of tomorrow."

The other three nodded. Then they ate in silence and retired to their rooms.

That same night, Ulises fell ill.

When they saw that his fever wasn't subsiding, they moved him from the loft into the room where Martín used to receive him. For five days, he couldn't get out of bed. On the morning of the sixth, Señora Carmen came in and felt his forehead. Ulises opened his eyes.

"Thank God," said Señora Carmen, smiling. "You're looking human at last. I'll bring you some broth."

Then he heard her informing the others that he was feeling better. Jesús came in.

"You gave us a fright. For a moment, we thought you were going to leave us, too."

"Was it that bad?" asked Ulises, sitting up in bed.

"You were delirious."

"I don't remember."

"Of course you don't, you were talking gibberish."

"Like what?"

"Weird shit. The weirdest bit was something about how there was a Nazi submarine going through your veins."

They laughed for a while.

"Well, it's over now."

"You're looking much better."

"Tell me, did anything get done in the last few days?"

"Everything's going like clockwork, don't worry."

"Any news?"

"Well, just a little thing with the lawyer. I don't know how he found out about Nadine, but he showed up here wanting to see you. I said no and he turned nasty. I had to put him in his place."

"Good for you."

"I don't like that guy. Best to keep an eye on him. Give him a call when you feel better."

"OK."

The next morning, Ulises went downstairs unaided for his first coffee of the day. The others saw him coming into the kitchen and smiled. They drank their own coffees in silence, as if nothing had happened.

"We need a meeting to get up to speed," said Ulises after a while.

That was when they heard a scream. Señora Carmen had gone to the front gate and was now running back inside.

"They've left another dog at the door!" she said, very worked up.

"Dead?" asked Mariela.

"Not dead at all. Alive, and very big."

"Who left the dog?" asked Ulises.

"I didn't see anyone," said Señora Carmen.

They went out to the main gate. They opened it a few centimeters, looked outside, and there he was. Ulises crossed the threshold and stood in front of the animal. The dog was sitting on his hind legs, his front ones straight, in a waiting position. He came all the way up to Ulises' navel.

"What sort of dog is it? asked Ulises.

"It's a Leonberger," said Mariela. "A German breed. They brought us one once, Jesús, remember?"

"Yeah, but not as big as this one," her husband replied.

Ulises rested his eyes on the dog, and the dog's eyes rested on him.

He felt an invisible and mischievous hand squeezing his heart.

"He's the biggest and most beautiful dog I've ever seen," said Ulises at last, patting the dog's head.

The dog stood up, slowly swinging the sail that he had for a tail, so that they could fully appreciate how huge he was.

Ulises noticed that he was wearing a collar. He sank his hand into the fur until he found a tag. It had a name on it.

"Iros," he announced. "His name's Iros."

34

The tag didn't have a phone number. Just that name they didn't even know how to pronounce. Ulises said Íros, stressing the first syllable. The others, Irós, stressing the second. A weird name, either way.

It starts with an *I*, thought Ulises. Just like Elizabeth's dogs.

A picture of Nadine flickered through his mind for a second, ethereal, then evaporated.

Mariela took some photos of the dog.

"I'll post these on social media," she said. "He's the foundation's first guest."

"We still don't know if he was lost or abandoned," said Jesús.

"Let's find out," said Ulises.

Iros appeared in the background of the image just before four a.m. The recording showed him walking down the middle of the street, like a mule on the edge of an abyss. He seemed tired, as if he had come a long way. He stopped twice to rest, before walking on until he reached Los Argonautas. Once there, he lay down on the sidewalk to wait.

"Poor thing. He's lost," said Mariela.

"I don't think he's lost. Look again," Ulises said, rewinding the tape. "He stops there, but not because he's lost. He's like a Bedouin in the desert, don't you think?"

Mariela and Jesús exchanged a glance.

"Don't post any announcements. If a dog like that is lost, the owners will contact us. Or they'll go looking for him everywhere. If someone claims him, and can prove he's theirs, well, then we'll give him back. But that's not going to happen. This dog's a godsend."

"Ulises, you can keep him if you want. We understand, in these circumstances," said Mariela.

"What circumstances? Come over here—tell me if that's the face of a dog who's lost."

They had tied Iros to the door of the bathroom near the kitchen, next to the stairs. They'd put out a dish of water that he had already drunk, leaving the bottom full of slobber.

Ulises held the dog's huge head between his hands and persevered.

"Look at these eyes and tell me if they're the eyes of a dog who's lost."

Iros raised his head panting. Like everything else about him, his eyes were huge. Two black, bottomless pupils with a slight squint. Mariela and Jesús drew near and touched him for the first time. Iros watched them calmly.

Suddenly Mariela's eyes welled up.

"Sorry," she said, laughing embarrassedly. "I don't know what's wrong with me."

"He does look calm, it's true," said Jesús with a lump in his throat.

Señora Carmen was listening from the kitchen as she chopped up a chicken.

"He's too big for the kennels," said Jesús.

"He needs to be out in the garden," said Mariela. "The question is how he'll get along with Michael, Sonny, and Fredo."

"Maybe he needs to be kept separately, in the dog cemetery, I don't know," said Jesús.

"We'll figure that out later. Right now I'm going to find out about the breed. What did you say it was?"

"A Leonberger," said Mariela.

"Leonberger," repeated Ulises, as he untied the dog and led him upstairs, leaving behind a trail of drool and earth.

Señora Carmen stopped what she was doing and took out the mop and bucket with soapy water that she always had on hand. She mopped the steps and within a minute, they were clean again. She looked up at the top of the stairs and after making sure Señor Ulises wasn't around, she whispered:

"Get rid of that dog."

"Take it easy, Carmen," said Mariela. "If he makes too much mess, I promise we'll help you with the cleaning until we can put him up for adoption. For the time being, it's good for Ulises. He seems happy."

"I know, but it's not that."

"What, then?"

Señora Carmen hesitated.

"Let's go outside," suggested Jesús.

Leonberg is a town in the German federal state of Baden-Württemberg about 16 km to the west of Stuttgart, the state capital. About 45,000 people live in Leonberg, making it the third-largest borough in the rural district of Böblingen, according to Wikipedia.

"We'll call you Iros Leonberg. That'll be your full name. Like Vito Corleone, you know? Oh, you don't? Well, we ought to have a *The Godfather* marathon soon. Let me finish up here and I'll introduce you to Michael, Sonny, and Fredo."

When they went down to the garden, they found Señora

Carmen, Mariela, and Jesús sitting at the table where Nadine used to spend her days reading Elizabeth and Altagracia. When the dogs saw them arrive, they ran over and circled around them.

"Go fetch the chains," said Jesús to his wife.

Iros seemed calm, but when he felt Sonny getting too close, he gave a hoarse growl that made the other three dogs turn tail.

At that moment, Mariela arrived with the chains, but by then, the dogs had already gathered at the back of the garden.

"He's going to hurt Sonny, either that or the three will end up hurting him," said Jesús.

"Don't worry. I've just decided I'm going to move back into the apartment. I'm taking Iros with me tonight, it's for the best," said Ulises. "I want us to weigh him and measure him right away. It says online, the average male Leonberger is between sixty and seventy centimeters tall. And sixty to eighty kilos. I have a feeling Iros is much bigger."

There was an awkward silence.

"What's the matter?" asked Ulises.

"Nothing," said Jesús. "I'm just not sure it's good for this dog to be locked up in an apartment."

"There's plenty of room in the apartment. And obviously I'll be taking him out twice a day. I'll have to take a bag of dog food with me."

"OK," said Jesús. "By the way, we wanted to ask if you'd like us to leave this table here or move it under the roof. It'd be in the shade if we move it back to where it used to be, and it's cooler there. But we didn't want to move it without asking you."

"Sure. Whatever you think best. So shall we weigh him, then? We need to think about vaccines too. How old do you reckon he is?"

By the time Ulises finally left that night for his apartment, they were all exhausted. Señora Carmen's wishes had come true almost magically, thanks to Ulises' decision, yet she was still anxious. After taking a shower, Mariela and Jesús lay in bed talking into the early hours, discussing whether they should go or stay. Mariela hadn't had any more nightmares but, like Carmen, she felt something bad was about to happen. She wanted to leave everything behind before it did.

Jesús thought they should hold on until the deadline set by General Ayala. If they managed to have everything ready on time, they'd be able to carry on with the foundation and in fairly good conditions, however bad things might be outside.

"Ulises isn't well," said Mariela. "Did you see what he was like today?"

"Yeah, he's all over the place."

"The only thing he talked about was the dog. Any other subject, you might as well have been talking to him in Chinese."

"We can finish the rest ourselves, Gorda. We just need to remind him to talk to the lawyer to make sure the stuff arrives on time. The difficult thing will be getting the foundation started by the deadline. From then on, everything else will be easier. We'll have the funding secured for five years, and after that, the house will be ours. That's what the General says in his letter. Just imagine. Who's to say things won't have gotten better in the country by then. And when that happens, we'll have our house, and a dog to give out to everyone who comes back. Because if things get better, people will."

"My love, it worries me you still believe in that."

"Believe in what?"

"That the country's going to get better, that people are going to come back. Or that this lawyer isn't going to try every trick in the book to kick us out of the house. What did Ulises say when you talked about him?"

"Well, I said the guy came around and that he was rude when he insisted on seeing him. And I told him to watch out."

"I can't believe you still haven't told him."

"Gorda, you can see how Ulises is. He's in complete denial about what happened with Nadine. To keep rubbing salt in the wound now, it's just cruel. What good would it do him to know that we saw the lawyer's car? And anyway, we don't know for sure that it's the same car."

"Oh, please, Jesús! Of course it's the same," she said, annoyed.

Mariela lay back and pulled the sheet up to her neck, turning away from him. Jesús switched off the bedside lamp. He had no choice but to tuck himself in, too, and turn over to his own side.

35

On their first night together in the apartment, they started watching *The Godfather*. Iros was more interested in sniffing around the rooms and corners of his new home than in watching the movie, but at least it was enough to give him a sense of the plot and the characters.

"It's always like that to start with," Ulises explained to the dog. "People pay attention to the main characters but not to the secondary ones. Which is fine—if you aren't clear about who belongs to the family, and especially who *doesn't* belong to the family, you won't understand any of it. But the thing about *The Godfather* is that the secondary characters are important. That's what I always used to tell my students: if there's one thing Francis Ford Coppola is teaching us, it's that there are no secondary characters in a good film. Any of his characters could, in an emergency—if I might put it that way—carry the plot on their shoulders. It'd be a different story, for sure, but still a story worth watching."

They watched parts two and three the following evenings.

To Ulises, Michael Corleone was a character every bit as deep as Hamlet. He watched the trilogy every year, and always felt anguish at not knowing how to answer the riddle that

Michael asks as he sits beside Don Tommasino's coffin: What was it that had betrayed him? His mind or his heart? When he pressed this point in his movie appreciation workshops, he could tell that the students didn't understand the importance of the question. Or that he didn't know to convey the importance of the question. Then he would be overcome with apathy, feeling ridiculous and hating his job.

After watching it this time, he was no longer sure that Ford Coppola's masterpiece was, deep down, a family story. In *The Godfather*, the mafia world was the frame for telling the story of a family, that much was undeniable. But this story about the family revolved around a problematic figure who was the real core of the movie and its multiple plots: the father figure.

Iros listened to his observations, and he would pant, wag his tail a little, look at him with those black eyes that seemed to come together like a pair of flying saucers or turn his muzzle the other way. And in each of these gestures there was such a depth of tenderness that Ulises felt they could contain all of his thoughts and emotions. As if on hearing him, Iros were saying: "I don't understand a word of it, but I love you. And I'd rather be here, listening to you without understanding, than anywhere else. Do you understand?"

Ulises did understand, which was why it was so difficult to leave him to go to Los Argonautas. In the meeting that they had after his convalescence, Ulises had given Mariela and Jesús the passwords to manage the bank account. That way they could handle salary payments and expenses for household and building work. Every week, Aponte transferred the equivalent in bolivars of a fixed sum of dollars. Ulises' duties were now limited to those of a chauffeur. So, all being well, the Simpatía por el Perro Foundation's headquarters would be ready before the deadline.

"We have three weeks left, according to Ayala's plan. We need to set the opening date soon, which I guess will be January 3, the last possible day according to the terms of the agreement. The only things still pending are the medical equipment, the medicines, and the sacks of food," said Jesús, unable to suppress his impatience.

"Has Aponte been in touch?" asked Ulises.

"Only that day when he insisted on seeing you, when you were ill."

"I have the feeling that man doesn't want us here," said Mariela.

"He wants the house for himself," said Ulises. "He's working for Paulina."

"Since when?"

"All along, I'm afraid."

"And why didn't you tell us?" asked Mariela.

"I only found out recently. Besides, I didn't want to discourage you. But I'll tell you something: I swear on Nadine's memory, we will have the equipment in two weeks."

"And how are you going to make that happen?" Jesús wanted to know.

Ulises took a sip of water and said calmly:

"I'm going to make Aponte an offer he can't refuse."

Why had he said that? What next? Was he going to grow a moustache and start using hair gel? And what about Nadine? Had he really needed to swear on her name?

Then he had announced with understated theatricality that he was going up to the loft and asked please not to be disturbed.

Señora Carmen hadn't touched a thing. Everything was just as it had been on the day after Nadine's wake, when they'd had to move him downstairs to look after him.

The fuchsia leotard hung on the back of a chair. He picked it up, smelled it, and put it back. He lay on the bed and rolled over to the side that used to be hers. On the floor, he saw the tome with Elizabeth von Arnim's works, next to the three manuscripts with Señora Altagracia's translations. He began to browse through them, just to see if he could find the hidden novel, but soon gave up. Then he tried to remember Nadine's body. The only thing he could picture was the scar. Ultimately, all scars are alike. Some are big and others small, some are straight and others crooked. That's all. Stripped away from the body, they are like keyholes without a door. Useless pieces that take you nowhere.

He checked the time on his phone. It had only been ten minutes. He couldn't leave so soon. It wouldn't look good. Ideally, he would sleep a bit. On his way out, he'd ask Señora Carmen to get rid of everything. Apart from the mattress, which was new. He'd take his suitcase of clothes back to the apartment. Although it'd be good if he could take the book and manuscripts, too. He'd figure out what to do with them later.

He checked the clock on his phone again. It was as if time had frozen. He thought about Iros, about his eyes, about those rough paws he would put on Ulises' arm to demand affection. About the golden and gray fur on his chest, which Ulises would rub up and down until both were left happy and exhausted.

There were still forty minutes to go. He felt sad at the idea of waiting all that time to be able to leave the loft, get in the car, and drive to the apartment where Iros was waiting for him.

These emotional outbursts, which could even overcome him when Iros was by his side, sometimes made him wonder whether the dog wasn't really a being sent by the devil. Whether the dog wasn't a herald of his own madness. He had loved Nadine with a fury that burned his skin. Amid the passion he felt toward her, toward her body and the beams of soul that radiated from her eyes, Ulises had emerged from within himself like a good snake, a glowing arrow that, thanks to her, had left behind the loose skin, the battered tissue of the prolonged neglect that his life had been until then. Hearing the news of her death, the horrible circumstances in which Nadine had died along with her husband and daughter, was like waking to his true existence, a husk waiting to dry up and turn to dust. And perhaps that's how things would have gone for those years he had left, yet the truth was, after those days of fever, Iros had arrived and wrought the miracle that only dogs can: that of substituting one love for another.

Nothing he had experienced before could be compared to what radiated from that gaze. Wasn't this love, then? Or love was, at the very least, a checkpoint on the way to an unknown land. What Ulises found in his dog's gaze, from the moment he first saw him on the sidewalk at Los Argonautas, was a land that begins where love ends. Peace and joy without the shadows. A mirror that had dropped its veil. The final edge of light before death.

There were still thirty-five minutes to go. Ulises got up. He shut the suitcase, picked up the book and manuscripts, and left.

36

Señora Carmen tidied the loft and disposed of what few belongings she found. Then she swept the floor and cleaned the bathroom. She filled a bucket with water, poured in a splash of lavender-scented disinfectant and mopped. She gazed out at the view of Caracas from the window while the floor dried.

She prepared Señor Ulises his meals every week, even though he hadn't asked her to. He just needed them to be kept in the freezer so he could take them out one meal at a time. Perhaps she had gone too far. That big dog reminded her of the other dog, but she hadn't noticed that the latter, Iros, had come after the tragedy, not before it. Nevadito, on the other hand, was like the foretelling of bad times to come. But had it been the poor dog's fault?

Carmen could tell there was something not right with that family ever since they moved in.

"Did they argue a lot?" Mariela wanted to know.

They were sitting at "Nadine's table," as they called it, next to the oasis of flowers, while Ulises read up online about the breed of the new dog.

"The general and his wife? Oh, loads. I didn't think they loved each other. Then I realized they did love each other, a lot."

"What about the children?"

"The twins were just starting college when they arrived here. You can tell they had them at the very latest possible moment. The general and Señora Altagracia looked more like their grandparents. They each did their own thing. Paul, the boy, was always very strange. The kid didn't even talk. He didn't get along with anyone. As soon as he finished his degree, he fled the country. He only came once a year. The girl Paulina also spent some time abroad studying, but she did come back. She was rarely seen after they got her an apartment."

The period that followed had been quiet, as close to happiness as there ever was in those days at Los Argonautas. The general and his wife began to spend more time with each other. The Señora let the garden grow wild and set up her studio in Paul's old room. The general, meanwhile, began spending his weekends at home, not going to those occasional gatherings of retired soldiers, where all they ever did was comment on the rumors of coups and countercoups within the armed forces. The gatherings of the Sociedad Bolivariana that he hosted in the library also became less frequent.

"It was just a group of old farts meeting to talk about Bolívar," explained Carmen. "Even older than me."

"What do you mean, 'to talk about Bolívar'?" asked Jesús.

"Just so. They used to talk, for example, about the Decree of War to the Death. How many times did they talk about it? I even learned the bloody decree myself. 'Spaniards and Canarians, count on death . . .'—something like that. So that bunch of old men, including General Ayala, would discuss the decree as if Bolívar had signed it yesterday. And they'd go on like that all afternoon. Those meetings made Señora Altagracia sick."

But soon afterwards, the fights resumed. Altagracia went

back to hiding out in her studio, or to performing endless tasks in the garden, while the general met his retired friends or the decrepit men of the Sociedad Bolivariana.

"They'd been looking for something for a long time. And now they seemed to blame each other for their not having found it," said Señora Carmen.

"Who did?" asked Jesús.

"The general and Señora Altagracia."

"And what were they looking for?" insisted Jesús.

"Who knows? For a while, it was the children. But after they had them, they realized it wasn't that."

"Did they ever mention anything?" asked Mariela.

"Not much, but you could tell. I wanted to have children myself, and I couldn't. God never gave me that gift. I'm not sure He gave it to the Señora either, but these days, with technology and money, people think they can cheat fate. The Señora persevered until she managed it, but it was too late, I think. They say that's why she had twins. They put all kinds of odd stuff in your head, right from when you're just a little girl. That you need to get married, you need to have children. And that's all well and good. But if it doesn't happen, so be it. Having children is not why you come into this world. You come here to love, whatever shape that might take. That's our only obligation to God."

One day, there was a massive argument. Señora Carmen never learned the cause. Altagracia used to shut herself up in her room for a few days after arguments like these, but eventually she'd always resume her routines. On this occasion, however, she stayed inside. And it seemed like this situation was going to continue until some later time—whether it was a few days later or a few years—when one of them would leave the house to go straight to the cemetery. It was then that, as happened with Iros, a big dog showed up at the door of Los Argonautas.

"Except that dog was brought by someone from the Caracas cable car. It was a gift to General Ayala from Señor Francisco."

"Segovia's brother?" asked Mariela.

"The very same. It was thanks to him that Segovia ended up here. After Señora Altagracia's death, General Ayala needed someone to help with the household."

"And why did he give General Ayala a dog?" asked Jesús.

"That I couldn't tell you. The thing is, the dog was so big and beautiful that Señora Altagracia agreed to leave her seclusion."

The dog destroyed the garden within a week. And one day he gobbled down the picnic Señora Carmen used to set up for the Sociedad Bolivariana gatherings.

"The general was furious and said he was going to get rid of the dog," said Señora Carmen. "It was a Mucuchíes. He'd lived in the mountains all his life, and the heat here was driving him mad."

Altagracia looked for a dog trainer. The Señora wanted to keep Nevadito, so she hired a trainer to come every afternoon. She remembered him as a nice boy. Very humble background. He was going through a rough patch so ended up living in the house for a while. The agreement was that he would help the Señora with the gardening in the morning, and train the dog in the afternoon. The boy got paid a fee for the training, and he paid for room and board with his gardening work.

"To start with, the general wasn't opposed to it, since the Señora seemed happy. The garden was gradually taking shape, and Nevadito learned some tricks. He even walked with them while they took care of the grass and flowers, so he learned not to destroy the garden. The thing is, what with one thing and another, Señora Altagracia, Nevadito and the boy ended up spending all day together."

"Did the general get jealous?" asked Mariela with a smile.

Señora Carmen, also smiling, nodded.

"How old was the boy?"

"A bit younger than Señor Ulises. And quite handsome, too."

"And Señora Altagracia, how old was she?"

"Señora Altagracia would have been seventy-something. Give or take."

"But that's absurd. That's like being jealous of a grandson," insisted Mariela.

"Yes, but that's because you never met Señora Altagracia. She was the most beautiful, most elegant woman I've ever seen. And now that both the general and the Señora are resting in peace, I can tell you, I think the boy did fall in love. The Señora, on the other hand, always saw him as a helpless kid. Besides which, by helping him out, she was also solving the problem of Nevadito and the garden. I think the general also saw that. Those two, except in matters of love, did understand each other completely."

"So why the jealousy, then?" Jesús wondered.

Señora Carmen smiled again before answering:

"The general was jealous of the dog."

37

They liked going to a park that was two bends up the road beyond the US Embassy. The other dog owners had been frightened when they first saw him, but after a while they understood that Iros was as shy as he was big, and that he only wanted to be left in peace. When he was in a good mood, he would play with a ball. Or he would roll around on the ground to scratch his back, kicking up a cloud of dust. Iros would go back home covered in so much soil, slobber, and dirt that Ulises had to clean the dog and then the apartment on a daily basis.

One night, after the painstaking general cleanup had been completed, they watched *The Dog*, the documentary about John Wojtowicz, the man who tried to rob the Brooklyn branch of the Chase Manhattan Bank on August 22, 1972. The robbery turned into a hostage situation that lasted more than ten hours and ended at New York's JFK Airport with the other robber, a guy called Sal Naturile, dead. The unusual thing about the crime was its motive. Wojtowitcz claimed he needed the money so that his wife Elizabeth, who had been born male, could undergo gender reassignment surgery. The movie *Dog Day Afternoon*, by Sidney Lumet, was based on this story. The funny thing was, on the day of the robbery, John and Sal went to a movie theater on Forty-Second Street to see *The Godfather* to psych themselves up. On their way out, Wojtowicz wrote the note that they would later hand to the cashier, which read: *We're going to make you an offer you can't refuse. Sincerely, The Boys.*

"Isn't that wonderful, Iros? Al Pacino played Wojtowicz, and John Cazale, Sal Naturile. The same actors who played Michael and Fredo Corleone ended up in the roles of the two crooks who'd gone to watch *The Godfather* like it was a tutorial for bank robbing."

The telephone rang. A message appeared on the screen: *Unknown caller.* Ulises answered.

"Time's up, Ulisito," a voice said, and then hung up.

He went on looking at the phone for a few seconds, and realized it was already December 20. Having Iros had messed up his sense of time. It'd soon be Christmas, then New Year's Eve, and with the New Year, the deadline: January 3.

"Ulisito."

He pictured himself putting a gun to the man's head, forcing him to call his contact at customs, but instead he connected the old Android cellphone to his computer with a USB cable and downloaded the *Aponte* audio file.

He didn't return the call, though. Instead, he signed up to an online forum on Leonbergers, and there he found detailed information about grooming the dog's hair and tending to his diet. Iros could go for two days without eating, and then recover his appetite without the least problem. Leonbergers had a very effective mechanism for self-regulation. Though Ulises did prefer to watch him gobble down his bowl and then, once they were in the park, leave a heap of excrement bigger than any other dog's.

The following day, he went to Los Argonautas. Jesús and Mariela had asked him to join them to go over the work so far. They went through the house checking everything. The kennels were all set up, just waiting for their guests. As for Severo, he had done a first-rate job with the electrical installation, the building work and the decorating of the walls and ceilings. The website still needed some attention, but at least it was live. Señora Carmen had ironed the staff uniforms. There were four uniforms with a cute puppy print and the foundation's logo on the chest.

"Why only four?" asked Ulises.

"Since we couldn't guarantee we'd be able to start on the third, some of the vets preferred to wait," said Mariela.

"Of course."

They took a quick walk around the second floor where they had fixed up a bedroom to be an extra consultation room, with a secondhand gurney that they had been given.

"This wasn't in General Ayala's instructions, but it all looked too empty," apologized Mariela.

"It's better like this," said Ulises, and he checked the time. "I've got to go. If I'm late taking Iros out, there could be some terrible disaster at the apartment," he added, laughing.

"Of course," said Jesús, unable to suppress a grimace of disgust.

When he arrived at the apartment, Ulises rushed to serve Iros his food. The dog devoured it faster than usual.

"Poor boy, you were starving. Come on, then, let's go to the park."

When they got back from their walk, Iros started to vomit. Or rather to retch, not bringing up anything but yellow drool. He was restless, pacing up and down the apartment. Ulises wiped away the drool and stroked him, trying to calm him down. Then he noticed, when he touched his belly, a strong trembling in his stomach. He called Los Argonautas and Mariela answered.

"Has he just eaten?" she asked, after listening to his symptoms.

"A while ago. He ate and then we went to the park."

"Did he eat a lot?"

"Well, he ate his fill."

"Did he run a lot in the park?"

"Actually, he did run a lot today."

"How long after eating did you take him out?"

"Straight away."

"OK. Best if you bring him here."

They took a while to get into the car. Iros was slow. He would stop suddenly to vomit, then he wanted to go back. When Ulises had finally gotten him onto the backseat, he drove out of the parking lot and over to Los Argonautas as fast as he could.

When Ulises had parked at the house, Jesús and Mariela came out to the car to take a look at Iros. He was lying down and didn't want to move. Mariela felt his stomach gently.

"How are we going to get him out?" said Ulises.

"I'm not sure we should. We haven't got what he needs here," said Jesús.

"So what do we do?" said Ulises.

"The ER at the San Román Clinic," said Mariela. "It's not the closest, but it'll be open for sure."

They all packed into the car as best they could and drove off.

Iros was suffering from gastric dilatation. Luckily, they had brought him in immediately since gastric dilatation, especially in dogs so big, could sometimes lead to complications.

Mariela explained that they needed to operate.

"Is he going to make it?"

"Of course, Ulises. Now that he's here, everything's going to be fine."

Two hours later, when Iros came out the operating theater, he saw him. He had bandages around his belly and was drowsy from the anesthetic. Ulises stroked his head and could no longer help shedding a few tears.

"I got scared," he said, apologetically, to Jesús, Mariela, and the vet.

"A scare is all it was," said the vet. "He'll spend the night here. We'll set up a special room for Señor Iros, because he's too big."

"Please put him in the presidential suite," said Ulises with a smile, wiping away his tears.

They got into the car and set off for Los Argonautas.

"Thanks, guys," said Ulises.

"You're welcome," said Jesús. "That's what we're here for."

"Seriously, don't worry. He'll be fine," said Mariela.

"It's so embarrassing," he said.

"Not at all! I wish everybody loved their dogs that much. Never be ashamed to cry over your dog," said Jesús.

"Oh, it's not just that. It's embarrassing that we couldn't take care of him at the house. At the foundation's own headquarters! I'll sort out all that crap tomorrow. I swear."

And this time, he was serious.

38

The business with the dog and his trainer could have ended in laughter, like in a Shakespeare comedy. However, as fate would have it, it was around that time that the twins came back home. Paulina was refurbishing her apartment, and Paul came from the US to renew some papers and get a visa to return to Europe.

"It was hell," said Señora Carmen. "The girl Paulina had a crush on the trainer, but he only had eyes for the Señora. And Paul was really annoyed with his mother for setting up her studio in his room."

Señora Altagracia began to spend some nights in her studio because of the recurring arguments with the general. After Nevadito's arrival, sleeping there became the norm. She argued that it was the room with the most powerful air-conditioning in the house, and it was where Nevadito slept best. No one would dispute that, though nor did anyone dare to ask why she also had to sleep in the same bed as the dog.

"The boy Paul became furious. We had to buy an extra bed. That's when they set him up in the small room on the second floor, the one where the general spent his last years."

Paul refused even to address his mother. He said she smelled bad and that she had let herself go. That she had gone mad.

"It wasn't true. The Señora smelled of dog, who she herself bathed once a week. And it's true her clothes were covered in dog hair. But that didn't make her mad."

The fighting became unbearable, and the trainer left, abandoning the garden only half-finished.

"I thought things would calm down, but then they took it out on the dog. I can understand the general not liking the situation, since it was his wife, after all. But the kids? Why get so worked up just because their mother slept with her dog? It was just nasty. They really made her suffer. And then came the dog's death, all so strange, and everything ended in tragedy."

At first, they thought Nevadito had run away. That someone had left the electric gate of the parking area open, the dog had gone out and hadn't known how to get back.

"The Señora was desperate. She printed little posters with the dog's picture and put them up all over Caracas. And look how nasty these kids turned out—that was the moment they chose to leave. Paulina said she'd rather stay with a friend, and Paul said his papers had all been sorted. And they left. After they'd tried their mother's patience so badly, they just left her in despair, all by herself. The boy never came back. Not even to his own parents' funerals."

Then a restless silence gathered around the house. General Ayala used to drive all over Caracas for hours, looking for Nevadito. Señora Altagracia couldn't stop crying. Until one day, walking around the back of the garden, she smelled it.

No one ever knew how the dog had managed to get through the railings, let alone discover that crypt-like place inside the mountain, but that's where they found him.

"And right there's where they buried him. So, in his way, Nevadito was the first to be buried in this house."

"And how had the dog died?" asked Jesús.

"Apparently the cave is quite narrow. I don't know. They say maybe he got in and couldn't get out again. Or that he broke a leg and stayed there."

"But, if that's what happened, they'd have had to hear him barking and howling, wouldn't they?" said Mariela.

"That's what the Señora said. After that, she locked herself in her studio and wanted nothing more to do with anything or anyone. I was the only person allowed into her room. I brought her food, changed her bedclothes, cleaned her room and bathroom."

"And what did she do?" asked Mariela.

"The usual stuff. Painting, but mostly writing. One time I asked her what she was writing. She said her memoirs. That she was telling the whole truth. That once she finished them, she would die. And that's just how it was. She took a whole pot of pills and died. I found her on the room's little patio."

"Did she finish her memoirs?" asked Mariela.

"I don't know about that. The general went out of his mind with grief. And guilt. He said he'd killed her. They had to commit him and everything. For two months. He wasn't the same when he came back. That's when he started picking dogs up off the street and he refused to let his children in the house. They started saying the general had gone mad. Imagine! Saying that about General Ayala, a man respected by everyone!"

"Did the general blame his children?"

"He never said so, not in so many words. But I think deep down he did. The general suspected that the twins had killed Nevadito. And once the dog was dead, the Señora didn't want to go on living."

39

At 6:45 a.m. on Tuesday, January 2, as the coffee grounds were just starting to emerge clearly at the bottom of the freshly emptied cups, the Los Argonautas doorbell rang.

"It's the lawyer," said Jesús.

They'd spoken to Ulises on the afternoon of December 24 to wish him a Merry Christmas. He apologized for not attending the dinner they had planned at Los Argonautas, but he was completely focused on Iros, who was making a slow recovery. They didn't hear from him after that, and didn't want to insist.

Mariela had been right to pack their suitcases, Jesús thought. He went to the intercom and lifted the receiver.

"Yes?"

"Good morning. It's Dr. Aponte," said a gravelly voice they could all hear.

Señora Carmen clutched her chest. Mariela didn't react.

"Give me a second," said Jesús, and he walked over to the front door. He opened it and went out to the entrance. He made his way down, step by step, measuring every movement. There was the garden with the dogs lying down in it, pricking up their ears when they saw him, and the table next to the flowerbed, which nobody had dared to move.

He crossed the paved path and opened the gate to the street. An older man, wearing a suit and tie, came toward him. Jesús smelled an exquisite scent he thought familiar.

"Good morning," said the man, giving him a firm handshake. "I'm Dr. Ariel Aponte, the executor of the General Ayala's will. Apologies for showing up so early and unannounced, but we're really coming up on the deadline now," he said, touching the glass of a very expensive watch.

Jesús noticed how the watch shone, and the old man's smile shone, too. And behind him, the two removal trucks.

"Are you here to take the stuff away?" asked Jesús.

"Take what stuff away? I came to deliver what was still missing. Hasn't Ulises said anything? Maybe he hasn't seen my message. Last night we managed to clear the equipment and everything else that had gotten held up in customs. May I come in?"

Without waiting for an answer, he gave the two trucks a wave and went into the house.

Jesús stayed where he was, while the two drivers and three assistants got out. They took out some barrows and proceeded to unload the goods.

Back in the kitchen, Jesús was met with a commotion from Señora Carmen, who apparently knew old Dr. Aponte already. Mariela looked at Jesús wide-eyed, as if demanding an explanation.

"We made it, Gordita," was all he managed to say.

Señora Carmen and Dr. Aponte stopped their chitchat for a second.

"We're so nearly there now," said Dr. Aponte. "Once the men finish unloading the equipment and the food, we'll have to inspect the premises and, if everything's in order, we still need to sign a heap of paperwork. Why doesn't one of you call Ulises and tell him to wake up and come over?"

"Right away," said Jesús and he grabbed the phone.

"Have you had breakfast, doctor?" asked Señora Carmen.

"A while ago."

"Just like the general. I would still be in bed, and he'd already have eaten."

"Discipline is something that stays with you. What did Ulises say?" asked Dr. Aponte.

"He whooped. He'll be here in no time," said Jesús happily.

"I don't blame him. Will you show me what you've done? So we can tell the movers where to leave the stuff, and we can save some time."

Dr. Aponte was very impressed with the alterations to the house that used to belong to his friend.

"More like a brother, really," he explained.

When Ulises arrived, he found them in the garden. Sonny, Fredo, and Michael had recognized Dr. Aponte. They rushed up to him, muddying the pants of his suit. The old man let them for a moment, and when they were threatening to get him dirty a second time, he shouted a command in English:

"Sit!"

And the dogs sat straight away.

"Martín was useless at training the dogs. I was the one who taught these rascals how to behave," said Dr. Aponte. He took a handkerchief out of his pocket and tried to wipe off the mud stains as best as he could.

"You got my message, then?" said Ulises.

"Yes, I did. We'll talk about that," said Dr. Aponte. "Now, we still have a lot of paperwork to sign. Shall we?"

They went back into the house and sat at the kitchen table, where Dr. Aponte had left a folder with the documents.

"These are the new documents for the foundation. The constituting regulations establishing roles and terms. And these other documents are about performance. Ulises, the papers for the apartment are in this folder here. Mariela and Jesús, these are for you. As Martín himself explained in his letter, there is a special clause: if the foundation remains active and efficient for the next five years, the house is yours. Please, check everything before you sign. While you do that, I'll see if I can find us something we can toast with."

"Isn't it a bit early for that, Doctor?" said Señora Carmen.

"Oh, that train will have left the station by the time they finish checking it all," answered Dr. Aponte, winking at her.

Ulises heard the old man's footsteps in the hall, demonstrating the same determination as his son, so vulgar and so different to his father in appearance and manners, yet so similar in those subtle gestures.

Dr. Ariel Aponte reappeared with a bottle of champagne.

"Let's pop it in the fridge for a while, Carmen. Is there any orange juice? We can while away the time until eleven and then toast with mimosas."

When the trucks had been emptied and the paperwork signed, they went to check how the clinic was looking with the equipment.

"Everything needs to be unpacked and hooked up by tomorrow. I'm guessing there'll be journalists, right?" said Dr. Aponte.

"The communications manager has sent out a press release. Only a handful have answered," said Mariela.

"So long as at least one person comes, that's something. I can't wait until eleven. I need to get going. Let's drink a toast," ordered Dr. Aponte.

They all prepared the drinks together. Dr. Aponte was in charge of the sober and heartfelt speech:

"To the Simpatía por el Perro Foundation—and to you, Martín, wherever you are. We honor you, old man."

Mariela pretended to sip from her glass and set it back down on the table. She couldn't hold back her tears. Their achievement in getting the foundation set up calmed the deep sea of her fears and produced an expansive warmth in her belly. That night she would tell Jesús the good news. Her body was a stronger omen than any past or future nightmare, and things were going to get better now.

Before he left, Dr. Aponte wanted to know what was planned for the garden.

"That was one of the things that worried Martín the most," he added.

"Well," said Jesús, "we think the best thing would be to leave it to the General's dogs. After that, when they're gone, we could look into building bigger kennels there. We'll see."

Dr. Aponte listened to his words attentively, and after a while he said:

"We'll need to think about whether it'd be a good idea to expand the capacity of the shelter. This is a place where the dogs should be happy, well looked-after and where they can find a home quickly. The key for it to work is to achieve a high turnover—I'm not sure I'm making myself clear. For it not to take too long for the little dogs to be adopted. That waiting is horrible."

He said this last thing staring at Ulises, his expression hardening beneath a sudden shadow of sadness.

40

Ulises preferred not to go to the opening. The only thing he wanted to do was to stay in his apartment watching movies with Iros. His plan was to switch off for at least a month, and postpone the future. One week later, however, Dr. Ariel Aponte called him and arranged to meet in his office.

Aponte was still excited about the work they had done with the foundation.

Ulises tried to play along, but he no longer felt connected to any of it. He scanned the walls with diplomas and the pictures on the desk, nodding along to Dr. Aponte's words. He was just counting the minutes till he could go back home and be with Iros.

Dr. Aponte suddenly broke off the conversation and said:

"Wanting to kill me! What do you say to that? I've always expected the worst from Edgardito but I wasn't expecting this, I have to say."

The old man was still smiling, but a crack had appeared in his gaze. Ulises responded:

"Sorry, but I don't follow. If you already knew what your son's like, why did you leave Martín's project in his hands?"

"I wanted to give him one last chance. Or maybe it was to

find out just how stupid he can actually be. I don't know. I'm glad that despite everything, you managed to get the job done. Martín was right about you."

Martín Ayala and Ariel Aponte met in the early 1940s at the Hijos de Dios Orphanage, in San José del Ávila.

"Martín was adopted when he was ten. I was seven at the time, I think. The couple were exiles from the Gómez dictatorship. Their son had died of a lung disease in Paris. When they arrived to collect Martín, he dragged me out to the reception of the orphanage and told them they had to take me, too. The nun doing the paperwork told him it was only him who was being adopted. And Martín, still holding my hand, said: 'We aren't puppies who can be separated just like that.' So they had to take us both. I did end up with another family, but that's the kind of thing Martín would do.

"Of course, we really were puppies. We're all dogs from the same pack. Orphaned, widowed and infertile, like El Libertador himself. The thing about orphans is knowing whether they are one of the good ones or the bad ones. I was unlucky in that sense. Did you hear about Edgardo? Now it turns out he's being investigated about some matter with one of those ghost companies."

"Is Edgardo adopted?" asked Ulises.

"Yes."

"And Paulina and her brother, too?"

"No. Theirs was an extraordinary case. Altagracia underwent a long course of fertility treatment. She had a couple of miscarriages before finally succeeding. And it was twins."

"So, Martín's children and Edgardo already knew each other."

"Of course, known each other since they were kids."

"I see."

"Ulises, there's no shortage of children in this world. The hard thing is having a father, but it's down to the children to find one."

He continued:

"Martín joined the army when he turned eighteen. That's where he met General Pinzón. I, meanwhile, studied law at the Universidad Central, where I met Dr. Arteaga, without whom I would not be here today."

Dr. Aponte pointed at the wall covered in diplomas and awards.

"Altagracia was wrong to be so insistent about getting herself pregnant. Paulina turned out to be a hyena capable of anything, and her brother, a zombie. And Martín was also wrong. Maybe that's why he bet on you. Now the apartment is yours. Martín also asked me to give you this."

Dr. Aponte handed him an envelope.

"A letter?"

Ulises found Iros asleep.

He had been slower and lazier since the operation. There were afternoons when he had to be dragged down to the building's small park to relieve himself. He didn't seem to enjoy movies like he used to, so Ulises began to read to him. He selected some of the best canine literature, excerpts that he would start reading and end up improving. The only text they read in its entirety was the "historical legend" of Nevado, El Libertador Simón Bolívar's dog, by Tulio Febres Cordero.

Febres Cordero's Nevado was a sort of Argos, but one who, instead of staying behind to guard Ithaca, had gone with Odysseus to the Trojan War. The story was more legend than history, but Iros didn't seem to mind. He watched Ulises intently as he read. And he panted when Ulises gave a lively narration of the text's epic highlights.

Iros woke up, lifted his huge head, and wagged his tail.

Ulises went to the en suite bathroom. He changed his clothes, picked up the green book of Borges's complete works, and went to lie in the hammock beside the balcony. Iros lay down next to him. That book was the closest he had to the *I Ching*. He would open it at random and start reading. This time, it happened to be one of his favorite stories: "The Immortal."

It's the story of a man who went off in search of the city of the Immortals and ended up running into Homer himself. He even realized at the end that he himself was Homer. The man is accompanied by a troglodyte who follows him around like a dog. At one point, the narrator says of his companion:

The Troglodyte's lowly birth and condition recalled to my memory the image of Argos, the moribund old dog of the Odyssey, so I gave him the name Argos, and tried to teach it to him. Time and time again, I failed. No means I employed, no severity, no obstinacy of mine availed. Motionless, his eyes dead, he seemed not even to perceive the sounds which I was attempting to imprint upon him. Though a few paces from me, he seemed immensely distant.

Ulises looked at Iros, who lay at his feet, focusing on some point in the universe.

Then the man dreams that the troglodyte finally speaks, and says: "Argos, Ulysses' dog."

Ulises fell asleep with the heavy book on his chest. He

dreamed that the Ávila was collapsing onto him. Like a sack of stones forever tumbling down onto him. At some point, under the rubble, he recognized the blue eyes of the cat, and woke up.

Iros was asleep. It was time to get him down to the park. Ulises tugged at his leash, half-affectionately, half-scolding, to wake him. He grabbed a little garden trowel and a plastic bag to pick up the heap of excrement he always left, and they went out.

When they reached the ground floor, the elevator doors opened, and they found themselves face-to-face with Paulina.

It took Ulises only a second to recalibrate the image. It was a man identical to Paulina.

41

Ulises hadn't known that his apartment had been the real home of Martín's family before they'd moved to Los Argonautas.

"I didn't expect to bump into you in the elevator. Let alone with such a big dog. That's the most beautiful dog I've ever seen."

Paul was identical to his sister, but nicer. His eyes were like Paulina's, which were like Martín's, which was confusing. But Ulises didn't see any of the zombie behavior that Dr. Aponte had mentioned. Rather he seemed discreet and well-mannered. While they walked the dog, Paul told him he had come to Caracas to visit his parents' graves and see the apartment for the last time before quitting Venezuela for good. And while here, to meet him, too. He was saddened by not having been around for the last years, as well as by the things that happened after his father's death.

"You'll know by now that our family is pretty peculiar. Or was. It's only Paulina and me left now. In any case, I think it's beautiful that Los Argonautas has become a dog shelter. If they could see it now, I think Mamá and Papá would finally be happy."

They were really more attached to the apartment, but for sentimental reasons, no more than that.

"This is the place we considered our home. Not the other one, which we never understood."

"That house changes when nobody's looking," said Ulises, and he told him about the vision he'd had at the library, with Segovia emerging from a secret room he'd never managed to find.

"Those two men had special powers," said Paul, smiling and giving his fingers a little shake. "It was Paco who gave me this bracelet. I went up to see him once. I had the idea of making a short film about the keeper of the Hotel Humboldt. I didn't make anything in the end. He told me that if I never took it off, I'd live to be a hundred. Even though I never met his brother, I was very sad when he died."

"How did you find out?"

"Edgardito told us. Later I learned that he acted very badly with you. And so did Paulina."

"Turned out to be a mafioso, that Edgardito."

"Oh, he always was. Now he's showed up on the board of directors of one of those ghost companies. I'm sure he's in hiding."

"And Paulina, was she always like that?"

Paul shook his head, sighed, and said:

"Not as much. It was because of Paulina we lost this apartment, actually. The whole thing with her getting married, it was only to upset the old man. To get him to react, so he'd at least put it under her name on the condition of her not marrying you. That really is what happened. But it backfired. I know that she loved you. At some point, she loved you. Not to mention my papá. He loved you like a son."

Paul revealed no strong emotion. He was a beautiful human statue.

"I didn't know anything about it. I didn't do anything to get Martín to make me his heir, I give you my word. Did the two of you get a fair share?"

"Oh, don't worry. Paulina got plenty. I didn't want anything for myself. I made that clear to Papá the last time I saw him."

Paul had wanted to be a film director. He was talented, and managed to enroll in the prestigious Prague Film School.

"I wanted to be Miloš Forman in those days. To make masterpieces. That kind of stuff. Nothing like Italian neorealism. Austere, hard, suffering films."

He ended up moving to Amsterdam, where he took creative writing workshops.

"I've been living there for years."

"Are you a writer?"

"No, I ended up in the bicycle business. In the Netherlands, motorized transportation has practically been replaced by the use of bicycles. There's an average of at least one bicycle per citizen. I was doing a bit of everything before setting up my own company a few years ago. I managed to develop a revolutionary concept in the industry, and it's been a success. Can't complain, really."

It happened on a boat trip on the canals while some friends were visiting. He was familiar with the tour, but he'd never previously actually paid attention to what the audio guide was saying. Two facts registered with him. The first, that the number of stolen bicycles in Amsterdam was somewhere between sixty thousand and eighty thousand a year. The second, that the maintenance services of the canals fished out around fifteen thousand bicycles a year. Paul immediately understood why the first figure had such a large margin of error. Many of those bicycles reported as stolen had actually fallen into the water.

Was the city council aware of this? That was his first thought. The next morning, at breakfast, he searched online and quickly found a few articles on the subject. The problem was more complex that he'd initially thought, since people did sometimes steal bicycles just to do one particular ride and then they'd throw them into the river. Paul ran the figures and estimated that the number of stolen bicycles, bearing in mind that many could be both stolen and *also* thrown into the canals, likely ranged from 65,000 to 77,500 a year.

Ultimately, all the articles he read revolved around the same enigma: how was it possible that more than fifteen thousand bicycles should end up in the canals every year? One of the theories was Amsterdammers' well-known fondness—and that of the Dutch generally—for beer. Many drunk cyclists fell into the canals. Yet, there was also an undeniable economic factor. Because there were so many bicycles in Amsterdam, they were priced much more cheaply than in other countries where people used cars. There wasn't much difference between repairing a bicycle and buying a new one.

The Netherlands was not only one of the most modern countries in terms of environmental legislation, marijuana consumption, and the regulation of red-light districts, but it had also achieved another miracle on a par with the substituting of automotive transport with bicycles: there were no abandoned dogs on the streets, nor any homeless people.

"Or at least, it's very rare to see them in Amsterdam."

Paul knew that there was a correlation between the excess of bicycles on the streets and the absence of homeless people and strays. Dogs were protected by strict laws against animal abuse. Meanwhile the homeless had refuges that provided them with food and shelter and where they were well looked after.

"Amsterdammers can afford to drop their bicycles wherever, get them stolen, or throw them into the canals themselves, and they do it not only because bikes are cheap or they're drunk or they urgently need to get someplace on a murky night. Bicycles are to Amsterdam what dogs are now to Caracas: the objects of its cruelty."

Paul went back to the canals and on his walks he refined a plan to tackle Amsterdam's bicycle problem.

By highlighting the inverse proportional relationship he had discovered between the lack of stray dogs and homeless people on the one hand, and the abundance of bicycles on the other, he wanted to make the Amsterdammers aware of the crime being committed against bicycles. One of his online searches led him to an article on "cyber ethics." This was a forward-looking branch of philosophy concerning the working conditions and the inherent rights of robots, entities that would increasingly be occupying the labor market in a technology-dominated near future. Why not have similar considerations aimed at expanding the concept of animal rights to cover inventions that somehow still anchor us to a distant past? Are the wheel and fire not presences so ancient that they have escaped the objectual-practical realm and become "spirits," in the original sense of the word? True "household spirits," like the bicycle or the coffee maker?

The scope of this *bicyclethics*, the ethics of bicycles, could be boundless. If the number of bicycles abandoned or thrown into canals dropped considerably, as Paul believed could indeed happen, there would be a slump in bicycle sales. That decrease, which at first would be seen as a contraction in the industry, could be capitalized upon by donating the surplus to those who couldn't afford them. Those donations would be rewarded with tax cuts. All of which would result in a drop in the number of thefts. As well as strengthening the exports of Dutch bicycles to the rest of the world.

"That's my invention: *bicyclethics*. And also the name of my consultancy business: Bicyclethics. In the end, I didn't become a movie director and didn't make any masterpieces, but none of what I've done could have been possible without cinema. Do you know what my inspiration for all this was?"

Ulises shook his head.

"Vittorio De Sica's *Bicycle Thieves*. That movie changed my life. It's absolutely gorgeous. Do you know it?"

"Of course! I've got it here. Want to watch?"

"Really?"

At that moment, Iros stood up, grumbling, and went off to sleep in the master bedroom.

Ulises found the movie in the Italian cinema section of his library. Then they settled down on the sofa in front of the TV ready to watch it, like two good brothers.

42

"I wonder what the boy's life was like," said Ulises.

"The boy? His name's Enzo Staiola. He made a couple movies then became a quiet Math teacher."

"How d'you know?"

"I know everything about Italian neorealism."

"I mean the character. How do you get over seeing your father like that? How do you escape such a terrible humiliation."

"With love, I guess."

Paul didn't sound very convinced.

"That wouldn't happen to Vito Corleone. If anyone dared to steal his bicycle, he'd be dead," said Ulises.

"Maybe, but most of us get our bicycles stolen, and there's nothing we can do about it."

The movie connected with one of Paul's greatest traumas.

"That intangible feeling that something's been taken away from you. Something very important. Maybe the most important thing in your life, even if you don't know what it is. I got used to that feeling years later. It's pretty common, according to my psychologist. But when I was younger, ever since I was a teenager really, I thought I was the only person with that stigma. Which is why I channeled all that anger and guilt toward my parents."

Prague had been a disaster. Followed by another experience with a New York film school, where he didn't even get accepted. That summer, Paul came back to Caracas to figure out what to do.

"I was in a really bad way. And when I went back to my parents' place, it was hell."

His sister Paulina was also back at their parents' while there was work being done on her apartment. His mother, Altagracia, now had a huge dog that kept the house in a constant mess. The dog had a trainer who didn't know a thing about dogs.

"He was in love with my mother. Or at least, that's what he said. A total hustler. But my father was the worst. He didn't want anything to do with anyone. He would disappear off to do his things only to come back shouting, which made us shout even louder, everything feeding into that family rage that spread like wildfire."

One afternoon, Paul was in his improvised room, since his had become his mother's studio. He was lying in bed leafing through a brochure about a creative writing workshop in Amsterdam. He got up to go to the bathroom and when he came back, he found the dog lying across the bed, making a mess with his muddy paws, brochure in his mouth.

"I went mad. I grabbed my belt and whipped him until he ran downstairs yelping. There was a huge commotion. My mother told me that if I ever touched the dog again, she'd kick me out of the house.

"I took one of the cars and drove off and didn't come back until the next day. When I got out of the car and walked to the entrance, Nevadito wandered over as if nothing had happened. He came over to me wagging his tail, and licked my hand. I couldn't believe it. I felt ashamed.

"Just like Christ, I thought. Always turning the other cheek.

Forgiving everything. With infinite love. I couldn't bear it. That's when I decided to kill him."

Ulises weighed up the words he had just heard. Outside, night had fallen. He looked at Paul's bead bracelet and thought about Señor Paco. How much longer would he live in his ship of stone? Who would go to his funeral?

"Of course, I didn't decide it then and there the way I'm telling you now. I've managed to process it after years of therapy. It was an unconscious thing. Like I was giving God a chance to prove His existence. To push me off a horse, the way He did with St. Paul, because I couldn't comprehend that such pure love could exist without offering a sacrifice, without guilt, or without punishment.

"And that unconscious force drove me to leave that huge pork chop bone in Nevadito's food that same night, when everyone was already asleep. I did it, even though I knew my mother was careful never to have any leftover food lying around. Or rather, I did it precisely because I knew it was dangerous, since my mother loved Nevadito so much.

"I got up very early, went to the garden, and confirmed that the dog was dead. I put him in a wheelbarrow and dragged him into a little cave I had discovered nearby years ago, in a hill in the Los Chorros Park. You know, that small mountain you can see from the garden.

"Two days later, I left the house. I couldn't bear to see my mamá like that. I went to Amsterdam and haven't been back since."

"Are you telling me all this now because you want me to kill you?" asked Ulises.

"It wouldn't be such a bad idea."

"We'd better watch another movie."

"What movie?"

"*The Godfather?*"

Paul looked at his watch.

"It's already eleven. And I can never watch just one part."

"We'll stay up all night, then. I'll take you to the airport. What time do you fly?"

"Seven in the evening. We'll need to stop by the hotel first to pick up my suitcase."

"No problem."

They watched the whole saga. Between movies, they prepared sandwiches and drinks, and talked for a long time. They fell asleep on the sofa around nine in the morning. Ulises would hold onto an image from some hours earlier, when dawn had begun to creep through the apartment windows, and he told himself that Paul was the strangest, smartest, most sincere person he had ever met.

They woke up shortly before midday. Ulises went to his room to take a quick shower and get changed. Iros was asleep on his bed. He lay down next to him for a moment. The dog opened his eyes and turned toward him. Ulises stroked his chest and the dog stretched out his four legs.

"Big ol' bastard," he said, planting a kiss on his ears. "I'll be right back."

Paul was staying at a luxury hotel next to Plaza La Castellana. Ulises waited in the car while he fetched his suitcase and checked out. Then they filled the tank at the gas station on the corner of Francisco de Miranda Avenue and drove off.

"Shall we stop at an arepera first?" asked Ulises. "We haven't eaten anything."

"Is the Rey del Pescado Frito still around? It'd be cool to eat there. We've got time."

"No idea, but we can try."

They entered La Guaira about one in the afternoon. Being a Saturday, there was some traffic, and it took them a while to make their way to the coastal road. The famous seafront restaurant was still open. They parked under a palm tree. Once they had sat down, they ordered grilled seabream, fried plantain, and ice-cold beer. They didn't talk much, focused as they were on savoring the food and looking out to sea.

Drenched in sunshine and salty air, Ulises thought the country deserved a second chance. He imagined the day when the dictatorship would fall, and the next government announced the reinstatement of the cable car between the Ávila and Macuto. He saw himself leaping over the mountain, thanks to the cable car, while the *Gnade* submarine left the Guaire riverbed through an underground cave to emerge in the Caribbean Sea, before entering the waters of the Atlantic Ocean, heading to Germany never to return.

He left Paul at the entrance closest to the Air France check-in desks. He would be flying to Paris then taking the train to Amsterdam. They shook hands and said goodbye.

"Thank you for everything, Ulises. Here's my card, in case you ever go to Amsterdam."

"Thank you, Paul. Have a good trip."

Ulises drove back with a strange feeling of peace. There was an accident near the Boquerón II tunnel, so it took him a little longer to get to Caracas. He couldn't wait to get home and lie down to sleep, hugging his dog.

Not even the echo of the words he and Paul had exchanged for more than twelve hours remained in the large room. Iros didn't come out to greet him.

He's taken over the room, Ulises thought.

He lay down on the sofa for a moment. There, on the glass table, among the DVD cases and coasters, he saw the bracelet of beads. Paul had left it on the envelope with Martín's letter.

He picked up the bracelet, holding it up between his fingers, and stared at it as if it were an insect. He grabbed the envelope, turned it over, and realized it was open. He put it back on the table.

He's going to kill himself, he thought, and put the bracelet on.

He didn't see Iros in his bed when he entered the room. He took two steps and found him on the floor in a strange position, his back to the door and his muzzle hidden in the narrow space between the bedside table and the wall.

In his fall, Iros had dragged down part of the duvet, which was stained with blood and vomit.

43

"Good morning, Mr. Kan. This is Dr. Ariel Aponte's secretary."

A few weeks after Iros's death, the news of Edgardo Aponte's suicide in the United States was made public. He was found in the bathtub of his Miami apartment, where he had bled to death. Ulises called Dr. Aponte to offer his condolences, even though it was a known fact by then that Edgardo had killed Iros. The security guard at his building had seen a Toyota Corolla pulling into the parking lot and the cameras showed Edgardo and another man going into the elevator.

Jesús and Mariela carried out the autopsy. Ulises learned that Iros didn't die of a new stomach complication, as he had originally thought, but that he was poisoned.

Dr. Aponte wasn't convinced by the hypothesis of his son's suicide.

"I'm going to carry out my own inquiries," he said. "I'll let you know if I find anything. And thank you for calling. I really appreciate it. Especially after what my son did to you."

The secretary had called to inform him that Dr. Aponte had the document for formalizing his divorce with Mrs. Paulina Ayala ready, and that he wanted to hand it over in person.

Dr. Aponte received him with a hug. Ulises recognized the

same perfume General Martín Ayala used until the end, even when he had stage four pulmonary emphysema and walked around in robe and slippers.

"I found your document of legal separation a few days ago, while going through Edgardo's papers. When I saw it hadn't been a year yet, I had to get on the phone and work a little magic with the dates. I don't know how come Paulina didn't realize that you were still married. That's something Martín didn't anticipate, and neither did I."

"Anticipate what?"

"Since the divorce wasn't formalized, Paulina could have claimed her share of the apartment that's now yours. The terms of the inheritance are quite definite, but a skillful lawyer like Edgardo would have been able to find his way around it and force you to reach an agreement, at the very least."

"Damn," said Ulises. "In that case, thank you."

"Not at all. But let's get back to the point. Little by little, I've been piecing the puzzle together—and so have you, I'm guessing."

Through Jesús and Mariela, Ulises had learned that the black Toyota Corolla belonged to Edgardo Aponte. It became clear to him then that Paulina was behind that first phone call from Nadine that prompted their reunion. The contesting of the will and the psychological autopsy were part of the same charade, just as Miguel Ardiles himself had warned him.

How had Paulina gotten in touch with Nadine? Ulises thought that maybe Nadine already had a relationship with Edgardo, one of many, as Señora Kando had intimated. When they launched the plan to recover the house, Paulina and Edgardo used her.

"It's not like she did such a great job anyway," said Ulises.

"She might have leaked them the odd bit of information. I remember how she convinced me a few times not to go to work at Los Argonautas."

Dr. Aponte listened attentively.

"It's also possible that, once she'd learned about the plan, Nadine then used Edgardo to get back in touch with me. Nadine was cornered, if I can put it that way. That would explain the sudden absences, the mood swings, the crying."

"And why do you think she wanted to be in touch with you?" asked Dr. Aponte.

"I don't know. To warn me. Or maybe she loved me."

Dr. Aponte smiled.

"I'm not saying that wasn't the case, Ulises. But I think you should know that Nadine, or María Elena, as she was really called, was $10,000 in debt to Edgardito."

"I didn't know that. But the last time we spoke she was really distraught. And I don't think she was acting."

"Well, maybe she felt guilty, precisely because she loved you and betrayed you. I think the final night she left Los Argonautas, she also met Edgardo for the last time and told him she couldn't go on. Maybe she made the mistake of threatening to tell you everything or to leave the house. The thing is, that same night, there's a record of a call from Paulina's cellphone to the phone of María Elena's husband. So far I have no way of knowing, but most likely she stirred him up by telling him things. Maybe even sending him revealing photos or videos of María Elena. The move worked out beautifully because that way she managed to kill two birds with one stone."

"Three birds," said Ulises thinking of Nadine's daughter, and he felt a headache coming on. "Paulina killed three birds. And with three shots."

227

"A tragedy. Well, that's my theory. There's nothing I can do about it anyway. What I would like to see is how she might get screwed back in the United States."

Dr. Aponte was trying to prove Paulina's involvement with the ghost companies his son Edgardo was going to be investigated for. In fact, the job Paulina had gotten herself in Miami was as Edgardo's front person.

"She must have realized Edgardito lost the house and the apartment because he was dealing with you behind her back. So she leaked information to the press to get rid of him. Now I'm investigating Edgardo's partner in Miami—ah, he's something else, too—who of course is screwing Paulina. I'm still working on it. I can't tell you any more than that. Has she gotten in touch?"

"Paulina? No, there's no sign of her. Do you think she'll come after me?"

"I could expect anything from Paulina, and we do need to watch out for her—but I think they've already hit you where it hurts the most. They did the same to their own mother, poor Altagracia."

Ulises thought about Iros and felt faint.

The entrances to the apartment had not been broken into. Aponte and his companion had the fob to open the doors to the parking lot and the apartment. They'd probably taken Nadine's keys. Or maybe she gave them to Edgardo herself. Is that why she was crying? Because on the night she left, she betrayed him, and there was no turning back. Maybe Paulina and Edgardo had planned to kill them both. Perhaps Nadine's husband acted faster than they expected and ruined their plan. Who knows?

Nevertheless, what really tortured Ulises was the thought that Paul had been somehow involved. What Paul told him about his life seemed sincere, barring one detail. In *The Murder of the Man of Wrath*, Altagracia claimed that Nevadito had been killed the same way as Iros, with poison. Except Altagracia didn't blame Paul, but Martín.

Reading Altagracia's memoirs had helped him to fill in some important gaps in the Ayala family portrait. That manuscript set him on the trail of certain secondary characters and stories. He had long chats with Señora Carmen and found the dog trainer's card in the files in Altagracia's studio. The trainer had moved to Canada, although he was still using the same email address. After much persuading, Ulises had managed to get him on Skype. He told him the story of the Simpatía por el Perro Foundation, all the way to Iros's death. Only then did the dog trainer speak. He confirmed the version of events narrated in *The Murder of the Man of Wrath*. He told him it was true Señora Altagracia had gotten in touch for one last favor: go into the cave in the Los Chorros Park, take some pictures of Nevadito's corpse, and bury him.

"Did you do it?" asked Ulises.

"I would have done anything for Altagracia," answered the trainer, who had preferred to speak with his camera off.

"And why the photos?"

"Altagracia wanted to know if Nevadito had been poisoned. And that's how it was, her children poisoned him."

"But how can you tell he was poisoned from the pictures?"

"I don't know exactly, but you have no idea what those twins were capable of."

The conversation had confused him, since it confirmed some of Señora Carmen's assertions, but at the same time didn't fit in with Paul's confession about the instrument of the murder, a pork chop bone, nor with Altagracia's accusation in her memoirs, where Martín was the culprit. Moreover, Señora Carmen had confirmed that Nevadito slept with Señora Altagracia in her studio. So how had Paul managed to leave the bone when everyone was asleep, if the dog wasn't even nearby? Also, how could he have known the bone would be so effective?

"I want to leave," Ulises told Dr. Aponte. "I want to sell the apartment and leave. Would you be interested in buying it?"

Dr. Aponte began to blink nervously.

"It's not a good time to sell right now. You know that."

"I don't care. I'll tell you what. Get a valuation of the apartment. Tell me how much you can pay and I'll tell you whether I agree or not. What do you think?"

Ulises and Dr. Ariel Aponte closed the deal by phone a week later. The apartment had been valued at $250,000. Dr. Aponte offered him $50,000. They agreed that he would give him ten grand cash in advance, and the rest would be transferred to an account he would open in his new country of residence.

"And where will you go, Ulisito?"

"To Amsterdam."

"I understand. Will you come to my office tomorrow? We can talk about your plans and see how I can help."

44

When he arrived in Amsterdam, Ulises booked a room in an aparthotel near Central Station. He would leave early in the morning and come back in the evening, exhausted from his errands.

"If you go to Amsterdam, you can ask for political asylum. I'll help you with the application form," Dr. Aponte had told him.

They organized a series of interviews about the Simpatía por el Perro Foundation, by way of providing life stories. In the interviews, Jesús and Mariela recounted the harassment they'd experienced after Thor's murder. Only, this time, Ulises featured in the story as one of the victims. Dr. Aponte had already begun to circulate information about Paulina's role as Edgardo's front in the United States, and her possible connection to his son's "suicide." For the application, it was essential to link Thor's murder with Iros's, and both of these with Edgardo's death.

Ulises submitted the application two days after he arrived. Then he opened a bank account and, as agreed, Dr. Aponte transferred the rest of the money from the purchase of the apartment.

When Ulises had managed to settle the most pressing issues, he could start going out for walks. On these first glimpses of the city, he confirmed what Paul had told him: there were lots of bicycles in Amsterdam, thousands of them, but hardly any homeless people or stray dogs. He grew to like wandering those streets of imperceptible bends that always took him back to a different canal. That geography, like a spilled glass beginning to dry, was an open-air version of the architecture of Los Argonautas, but without the shocks.

He enrolled in free Dutch classes organized by the local council. A student with no prior knowledge of the language could acquire reasonable familiarity in just two years. Two years in which he'd wander the City of the Immortals, like a troglodyte, thought Ulises, like the only stray dog in Amsterdam, until he was ready to utter his first words in a dream.

He had been in the city for a month when, on one of his walks, he stopped at a long line of people waiting outside a small gray building at Prinsengracht 263. He realized it was Anne Frank's house and joined the line.

Learning the history of the place was heartbreaking, though Ulises couldn't help but think it was the perfect location to shut yourself in and write. Anne Frank's "Secret Annex" as a version of the cave imagined by Frank Kafka, who was her real father, not Otto Frank, as Philip Roth had already discovered. He liked the museum gift store because they didn't sell fridge magnets or coffee mugs of Anne Frank's face. The only thing they sold there, apart from postcards, was the *Diary*. They had it in about twenty languages and different formats. Ulises bought a copy in Spanish and a postcard, thinking he might send it to Don Paco, although he knew he never would.

He remembered Martín's last letter, which he had carried with him since leaving Venezuela. Martín's letter and Paul's business card.

Spuistraat 303.

He had memorized the address. Apparently it was opposite Café Zwart, a famous writers' hangout.

He felt the weight of the letter and the card like two stones in his coat. Leaving the Anne Frank Museum, he decided to take the streetcar into the center. He found an empty seat, sat down, and searched inside the top pocket of the old coat Dr. Aponte had given him. It was too thick for what little cold still hung in the May air, but it protected him.

He took out the sheets of paper, which folded and unfolded to the touch, like a well-trained flower, and read once again:

Dear Ulisito,

If you are reading this letter, it's because you've successfully set up the foundation at Los Argonautas. Congratulations. Now, if you've made it this far, it's because you've also managed to navigate the sea of shit that surrounds me, or that used to. At this stage, I don't need to explain who those two fertilized monsters Altagracia and I spawned really are. So, apologies if you've gotten splattered by any of this. I hope it wasn't too bad. You can reproach me for not warning you about anything, not about the inheritance, nor about what awaited you—but the truth is, I got a real childish enjoyment from writing this will. One should leave this world with a clear conscience at having given the best of oneself, but I'm not going to deny it's also appealing to leave a pigsty behind.

I don't know why I'm being so scatological in this, my last letter. One is meant to use these occasions to say loftier things. Like Goethe, for example: "More light." To tell you the truth, what I fancy shouting is: "More shit." What can you do. Maybe this is my way of rebelling against death. I've been fearing death for years. When you suffer from pulmonary emphysema, life feels like a faucet of air that's slowly turning off. It's as if every word you say, every walk you take, every burst of laughter you let out or sudden fit of rage, are a dose of air escaping the small tank of oxygen we're given when we come into this world. Mind you, now I think about it, it's the same for everyone. At least the emphysema sharpens your hearing, so you do notice the faucet being turned off. There's nothing more horrible than dying without realizing it. Without experiencing that last, eternal second.

I guess you've had enough time to keep exploring the library. Don't expect me to explain anything that happens there. It's a mystery to me, too. Maybe you've paid more attention to the gallery. It was assembled by General Pinzón following a catalogue published by the Quinta de Anauco, the house where Bolívar lived and where the original collection of El Libertador's portraits can be found. When I bought the house, I only took down one of the portraits. The one of Don Juan Vicente de Bolívar, Simón's father. Have you read anything about the guy? A son of a bitch of the worst kind. A tyrant, and a reprobate. Best thing he did was fathering Bolívar and dying when his glorious younger son was not yet three. However, in those few years, young Bolívar assimilated all the resentment that can fit into an orphan's soul. And with that resentment, the hero built his legend and, while he was at it, that of Latin America. Bolívar was an orphan, a widower, and infertile. And that is our father. We are the seeds of that desert.

Lately, I've begun to wonder if Bolívar believed in God. Nonsense, I know. It's like wondering if God believes in God. I've spent years of my life trying to understand El Libertador's

personality. At first, I was fascinated by his career in the mili-
tary. Then, his erotic exploits. After that, his moments of terrific
lucidity when he would realize that nothing made sense. I
went through all these stages and kept looking for what I hav-
en't glimpsed yet: I was searching for a trace of blood in the
cracks of the statue. But that trace doesn't exist, Ulises. In all
the battles Bolívar took part in, he didn't get a scratch. At least,
historians don't record any. Neither do his letters. Don't you find
that strange?

Even though I didn't find any blood at all, I did discover
something better. Something worth more than all the spilled
blood: a teardrop. In the box Segovia gave you, you will have
found Tulio Febres Cordero's chronicle. From a literary point of
view, it's a dreadful piece of writing, but every time I go back
and read it again, I end up crying. That's the truth, Ulisito.
That moment, just after the final victory has been secured in the
Battle of Carabobo, when the Native Tinjacá tells Bolívar: "Ah,
my General, they have killed our dog!" That's when Bolívar sees
the dog pierced by a spear. The snow of his back stained with
blood. And that's when Bolívar realizes the cost of that war. "He
watched the sad scene in silence, motionless like a statue, and
suddenly twisting his horse's reins with a pained, spiteful move,
he rode violently away from that place. In his eyes shone a tear
of fire, a tear of boundless sorrow."

Of course, no one believes in that story nowadays. But we'd
be better off if we did, we'd be better off imagining that little
tear sometimes, just the one tear, and we'd see how things begin
to change. Because nowhere else in the history of Venezuela, on
no other page of the thousands written about the life of El Lib-
ertador, will you find that tear. Some might say Tulio Febres
Cordero wasn't a great writer. Maybe so, but I don't know any

other in our literature who has drawn tears out of a statue. And if drawing tears out of stone doesn't make you a good writer, well, I don't know what does.

I don't know what I'm saying anymore. By the way, I hope you are reading this letter lying in bed, with Nadine by your side, asleep. She's such a sweet, silky girl. If that's not the case, you're a jerk, Ulisito. Either way, if it makes you feel better, I don't believe our country has much time left. All that wickedness with the dogs, God's poor little children, can't be left unpunished. We don't deserve another chance.

Don't ask me, not that you can anymore, how I know all these things. Supposedly a father knows, or should know, more than his children.

Martín.

45

He got off the streetcar at the stop suggested by the app, walked a few steps, and found Spuistraat. In the distance, he could see the front of Café Zwart. There, he sat at a table on the terrace, almost on the edge of the sidewalk. Opposite was number 303, a brick building with a bookstore on the ground floor.

He ordered a coffee and as soon as the waitress had left, he saw him approaching. He had on a short coat and a light scarf, more like a colorful foulard. A hat à la Gay Talese covered part of his face, but Ulises had no doubt that it was him. He carried a bag from the Albert Heijn supermarkets, and another from the Athenaeum bookstore. From far away, and in those clothes, he looked like Alain Delon in *Le Samouraï*.

Without looking round, Paul climbed the building's front steps, put a key in the big old door and went in.

Ulises leaned forward a little on his chair to look up at the third floor.

Had Martín killed Nevadito, as Altagracia swore he had? Or was it Paul, as he himself confessed? Had Altagracia fallen in love with her dog? Who was lying? The father, the mother, or the son? Or was the truth of this family really a blind spot for him? Was that what a family was about? A series of agreed assumptions one shouldn't talk about in front of strangers? Had Paul lied to clear his father's reputation, or his mother's? Or was it a warning, did he still insist that God would push him off his horse, like his saintly namesake?

His neck began to ache. A yellow light went off upstairs. Ulises could make out the silhouette, still wearing the coat and hat, and his features in the darkness, highlighting the blue of his cat eyes.

Paul moved away from the window and the light went out.

Ulises took out his phone and saw the news. In the small hours of the morning, Venezuelan time, an uncontainable fire of unknown origin had engulfed the Hotel Humboldt. There were already videos online showing the hotel burning like a torch in the high Caracas night. Like a rocket that explodes before liftoff. By early morning, the situation was threatening to get out of hand, as rumors spread that it was in fact the eruption of a volcano which, as the legend had it, had always been asleep in the entrails of the Ávila.

Don Paco, he thought. Hopefully he went down with his ship.

Ulises also thought about Nadine, the *sweet, silky girl*, in old Martín's words.

He felt something itch on his wrist. He pulled the bracelet up at the top and the beads back fell with perfect symmetry onto the two sides of the thread.

The waitress brought his coffee.

Ulises Kan downed it in three sips that burned his tongue. He had a good look at the signs drawn at the bottom of the cup. Then he stood up, left some coins on his table at Café Zwart, and walked away.

Acknowledgments

I would like to offer my sincere thanks to the following people, whose valuable comments, corrections, and suggestions made this manuscript into a book: Gustavo Guerrero, Jorge Manzanilla, Pilar Reyes, Pilar Álvarez, and Carolina Reoyo.

And finally, I would like to thank Noel Hernández González and Daniel Hahn, since it is a novel's translators who are its last true editors.